FRESH

Anthology

First Montag Press E-Book and Paperback Original Edition October 2017

Montag Press
ISBN: 978-1-940233-45-1
Cover design © Niall Gray
Cover artwork © struckdumb (https://struckdumb.deviantart.com)
Editor – Zachary Amendt
Managing Director – Charlie Franco

A Montag Press Book
www.montagpress.com
Montag Press
1066 47th Ave. Unit #9
Oakland CA 94601 USA

Printed & Digitally Originated in the United States of America
10 9 8 7 6 5 4 3 2 1

"[A] bit radical, a bit madcap ..."

— *Kristine Fisher*

"[K]ept my attention rapt from start to finish ..."

— *David Styles*

"[T]he complexity and diversity of the characters creates a range of reactions during reading, [allowing] each tale to shine on its own merits ..."

— December Cuccaro, *Heavy Feather Review*

"Every character ... feels like someone you might've known in real life."

— Anna Codutti, *Tulsa World*

"Beautifully written with not a foot put wrong ..."

— A.J. Hayes, *Lux: The Road to Calithia*

Contents

Foreword

Our wine merchants won't tell us the pejorative they privately use for trendy, flavorless vintages: 'crowd-pleasers.'

Veuve Cliquot, too, is 'Agent Orange.'

As a cross-section of literature, the choicest cuts, our FRESH anthology succeeds exactly where other big-ticket, celebrity-edited, highly touted emerging writer collections stumble. In that, here are the finest stories we could find across all genres – and the result is an electrifying solera from talented writers.

Including one of my own. A curator has his prerogatives.

Zachary Amendt
Menlo Park, CA
June 2017

Framers of Our Constitution

Gray Oxford

"Has the world changed or have I changed?"
- Steven Patrick Morrissey

On the third floor of Metropolitan Museum of Art is a 19th Century replica of a Parisian dining room located in proximity to the Eiffel Tower. The channels of cherry moulding and a centered fireplace configure the room into a monument bon vivant, yet, like a silhouette limited only to its form, these channels, this custom moulding, once traced men who occasioned the moment - rarely the monument.

Painted on the surface of each dining room wall is a blurry pink and blue homage to Monet impressionism. As my friend Zena described, "it's Claude(y) with a chance of grape". The walls void of scenes, landscapes or images provided canvas for residents and resident guests engaged in the trial and error of their own impressions to the room.

In between buttered meals, buttery soup and Chardonnays, with their heads tilting, conversations of categorical insignificance furnished drafts sufficient to propel the windmills. This was the mechanism of cosmopolitan life.

A thorned sadness in the side of my throat pained at the thought that perhaps the owner of this dining room (who goes nameless in this exhibit) would rather the walls had provided comfort over comport, introspection over indigestion, and texture not conjecture. This room was not conceived nor built by an invisible hand or invisible heart. It was dreamed, and it was built, and it was art.

The Chairman of The Board

Christopher Connor

The price of beef was down. They'd been saying it inside the bars and along the fences in the Elkhorn Valley, and every rancher seemed to carry it on his shoulders. It was a constant subject of conversation at the post office and inside the bars, and the underlying theme to every anecdote at Robert Cahill's house, where the ranchers gathered frequently during the winter for "board meetings." Because Robert was the host, they called Robert the Chairman of the Board.

They called Jack the City Boy. He did not, like the other men at Robert's table, own a ranch. The price of beef did not matter to him. He had a life away from the valley, but he was Robert's best friend, and visiting the ranch was his only release from private gripes of city life. Attending the board meetings appealed to Jack, but drinking before noon on a Monday morning did not. He fake-toasted when Robert stood up to make some proclamation about everyone's health, just as the phone started to ring.

They toasted bourbon, but the dining room smelled like a cocktail of tobacco juice and manure. Eight men halfheartedly held up their glasses. Just three years ago, eleven families owned cattle ranches in the valley, last year it was nine, and now eight. Their glasses clanged against the table.

The ringing continued. Jack excused himself to the kitchen, hoping for a moment of calm amidst the calamity. Robert's wife,

Susannah, leaned against the kitchen counter, slowly thumbing through a magazine.

"The phone?" Jack said.

"It's not for me."

As soon as Susannah spoke, the ringing stopped. She looked up at Jack and smiled with satisfaction.

"Did you hear about Nathan?"

"I did. Some cyber security job in Seattle, right?"

"Something far over my head, but it's good. Real good."

Again, the phone rang. Robert cursed loud enough for Jack to hear and trundled into the kitchen, breathing heavily between coughs. He spoke into the receiver, cursed, hung up the phone, and returned to the dining room.

"You boys having fun?" Susannah said, still not looking up from her magazine.

"No more than usual."

"It's getting worse, you know."

Jack knew.

"Talk to him, Jack, if you can. He's starting in the morning now, and it goes all day. If you can."

He smiled at her, and walked back to the dining room. The ranchers at the table had shifted their conversation to complaints about Miles Stainbrook, who had become the gasoline that powered their outrage at outsiders when he bought two ranches in the valley from families who had owned them for generations.

Robert was no longer sitting at the table, but standing and buttoning an overcoat.

"Robert? Everything OK?"

"Lester here," he said, motioning toward one of the other cowboys, "his hand just called to say three of my cows were spotted up near the base of the mountains on Forest Service land."

"I'll help," Jack said.

Jack possessed exponentially less experience than the other men sitting in the dining room, but he was sober, and everyone else knew it. Robert nodded, and started for the door. Jack followed, stepping out of the toasty house and into the Montana winter. Banks of charcoal-colored clouds were collecting above the western horizon.

They traversed the edge of Robert's ranch on the public access road, heading toward the barn. Wind knocked against the windows of the pickup, joining the sound of rocks kicking up from the tires and Robert repeatedly spitting into a plastic bottle.

"How them uppity law bastards treating you in the real world?" Robert said. Jack smiled to himself, but continued to look out the window.

They first met in law school, though Jack was five years Robert's elder, five years of working double shifts in the copper smelter for tuition money. The grit of the smelter was still caked under Jack's fingernails when they first shook hands. They'd practiced law together briefly after graduation until Jack landed a high-paying job in Helena. Robert came back home to the family ranch, law diploma thrown into a box in the attic once his father couldn't run the ranch alone. Robert came back like the other boys of the valley did. The old ranchmen of the Elkhorns, surnames hanging above arches to dirt driveways and initials branded into the side of the cattle, were long buried in a decaying cemetery next to the whitewashed church at the edge of town, their sons now the holders of the land, growing older and assembling in the Cahill dining room for board meetings. A cyclical life, until one day it's not.

"Susannah was telling me about Nathan. He's big time now."

Robert hit the brakes. A black crewcab truck pulled up alongside them on the narrow road, sped up, and hit its brakes. Robert stopped and pulled over.

"This asshole," Robert said between spits.

Miles Stainbrook stepped out of the black truck and waved. He walked toward Robert's truck, the metal tips of his bolo tie flapping in the wind. To Jack, Stainbrook always appeared five years younger than the odious man described by the other ranchers.

He reached Robert's window and knocked, lifting his round glasses onto the top of his smooth head.

"Robert, good thing I caught you."

"I have nothing to say to you."

"I heard there are some cows loose north of your ranch, might want to check if you're missing any."

"Piss off, Stainbrook."

"Well I also wanted to remind you of where to come if the bank's still on you."

Robert spit tobacco juice at Stainbrook's feet and Stainbrook took two steps backward.

"You want this land, you can pry it from my cold dead ass," Robert said. He revved the truck engine and turned back onto the road, nearly hitting a fence as he swerved around Stainbrook's truck. Around another tight corner, grinding the transmission, the truck skidded to a stop in the gravel driveway in front of the barn.

Jack stepped out of the truck, and felt the air burn the back of his skin. The wind whisked beneath this scarf and bumps formed on his neckline. Snow, and soon.

He didn't know what to expect. He enjoyed being invited to the board meetings, to feel like a member of a club to which he assuredly didn't belong. He loved when Robert asked him to help on the ranch, and usually he jumped at the idea, but as word of missing cows clouded the air, he wondered when Robert last inspected his herd. His stomach cramped, kicking him from the inside. His gaze turned to the building clouds.

Previous winters, Robert would have known the exact number of cows in each of the pastures that dotted his 3,000 acres of ranchland at the foot of the Elkhorns. Previous winters, he would have known the count of all the expectant mothers in the pastures. He would have ridden through the herd each day. Previous winters, he would have seen a break in the fence, and the two men would not have to ride into the mountains searching for pregnant cows while Montana threatened to freeze the blood creeping through their arteries.

Robert led Annie from the pen behind the barn. A dark grey mare, Jack had owned her for a decade, and paid to board her at Robert's ranch. Her shoes had been removed at the beginning of winter, and he expected to leave her out in Robert's fields until branding season, but Jack was a part-time cowboy, a weekend helper with one horse and one option. The thought of the storm shivered the wrinkled skin beneath his jacket. He had to use her.

Robert stood with Lucy, a three-year-old quarter-horse he'd bought the previous year and paid the Carter boy down the road to break her that summer. He brushed her, whispering in her ear as his calloused fingers caressed her shoulder before lifting his worn leather saddle onto her back.

"You sure you want to use her today? It's going to be hard out there without shoes."

Robert treated Lucy differently, caressing her neck gently before he saddled her. After thirty-three years of friendship, Jack knew Robert saved his intimacy for his favorite horse. But in December, the dirt ground of the valley was frozen solid. As the land crept toward the base of the mountains, frosted soil turned to rock. Holes burrowed by badgers and gophers lay stealthily among the stones.

"We need to get out and back as soon as we can. Weather's coming, and she's the best damn horse I have." Robert lifted himself into his saddle, struggling to put pressure on his left leg in the stirrup.

He rode up next to Jack, leaned down, whispered into Lucy's ear once more and gave her a pat on the side of her neck. Spurs to her flank, he started north toward the mountains. Jack followed. The cows in surrounding pastures stood restlessly, mooing together in off-key harmony. From the inside of his coat, Robert removed a flask etched with his initials and passed it to his friend.

In the earliest stages of their friendship, Jack realized that it was easier to take a nip off Robert's flask than to argue about why he wouldn't. Now, he took a small one, knowing he still hadn't found the right moment to say something to Robert about the growing evidence of a problem, even with the earlier prodding from Susannah.

The horses kept a slow trot, the wind rustling underneath the flaps of Jack's scotch cap. He looked at Robert, wearing only a cowboy hat, his ears turning crimson against the dull palette of the landscape. Robert the full-time cowboy, trying to prove his toughness against the nature of his own land. Jack held his reins tightly in his gloves while he huddled on his horse, waiting for the whiskey to warm him.

"You know the Carter family down the highway a bit? Their oldest son, Harry, he caught a DUI last week. He didn't want to say anything about it in front of everyone else."

"Is that his third?"

"I think so. They were wondering if I could help Harry out on the charge. But you know I'm not in the Bar anymore."

"I can take care of it," Jack said.

"I could give you a half a beef for helping." Robert took a large swig from the flask and handed it over to Jack. "I owe'm as much for giving me extra hay for the winter."

"A quarter would be plenty. Send the other quarter out to Nathan in Seattle, help him out a little bit." Another sip, and Jack felt the muscles in his neck relax.

"Like I said, I think we could do half a beef for your help."

The mountains ahead, spotted green and brown at the base, were capped with heavy coats of white near their peak. A late

December snow had melted in the valley, but the snowpack in the Elkhorns remained firm. As he stared at the frozen summits, Jack wondered how many cows could have escaped, how far into the wilderness they'd wandered.

Four winters ago, he and Robert helped Lester Anderson search for a heifer in the same stretch of mountains and Jack was bucked off into powder when Annie stepped in a badger hole. She survived, leaving him sprawling on the ground, shivering. Now, he watched every step she took in between glances at the weather-stripped fencing of the pastures.

"What Stainbrook was saying earlier, about the bank," Jack said.

"Don't listen to him."

"I'm not, Robert. Susannah said something to me about it too, maybe two months ago."

"I'm not selling my great-grandfather's ranch, not to some damn outsider. I get too old, my boy will come back. Watch out for those cows."

"I'm looking."

"If one of them gets lost out here and has problems with her labor, I lose a calf. Price of beef was bad enough this year. I can't afford a single stillborn."

The men turned east, searching for a breach. Jack's stomach tightened. He grasped for encouraging words for Robert, but came up empty. Without his family's land, Robert would lose his meaning. He knew Robert knew it too, but didn't know how close his friend was to the edge.

The two friends neared the ranch's northern fence. Lucy and Annie stepped carefully among the rocks. The wind picked up, whipping in fierce circles.

"There," Robert yelled, Jack just a few feet to his left. Two outer fence posts were pushed into the ground, wire tamped into the frozen earth at the edge of one of the pastures.

Robert straightened in his saddle and looked back toward the barn. "This hole is an easy fix, but we need to find the missing ones before it snows. I'll do a quick count, see how many are gone."

Jack nodded. He watched Robert ride through the maze of pregnant cattle, some close to birth. As Robert neared the far end of the pasture, he took a slow sip from the flask before he turned and rode back to the break.

"I'm only missing the three," Robert said. "I think."

The last two words blew around Jack's cap and stung the inside of his ears. He should know the count, Jack thought. He should know.

The two rode over the trampled fence and tried to follow the easiest route into the Elkhorns.

"You're lucky you only lost the three," Jack said. He wondered if it was the only hole at the ranch. Robert could have lost the whole herd.

"If I had enough help around here, they'd already be back."

"You have me. You know I can help." A sincere offer, begging to be asked. Two weeks earlier, Jack's boss laid out his future. Half-time, partial retirement. He could start pulling Social Security. Only a slight net loss in income. The money wasn't his problem, only the time. The twenty hours of work that would disappear each week into time spent sitting at his house. Inaction frightened him.

"On the weekends, Jack. I appreciate it, but I need someone full-time. Getting to the point my daddy was at when I came back."

Jack heard the sound before he saw them. A sick mooing echoed off the Elkhorns and careened through the trees. Not the sound of a cow speaking, but tinged with the urgency of a child calling out in the dark after a nightmare. Jack struggled to place its location.

Robert turned his horse northeast and spurred her to a gallop. The forest approached like an avalanche. Lucy darted between the trees. Annie struggled to keep up. The forest thinned into a small clearing. Three cows huddled in the middle.

Robert jumped off Lucy and limped to the cows. Two lay on the ground, the third standing and mooing loudly. Robert ran his hands from the top of her shoulders down to her rump.

"Damn it, Jack," he cursed into the wind.

"Looks like she's carrying low."

"She'll go into labor any time. She's early."

Robert yelled at the other two cows and roused them to their feet. He gave each a quick, careful examination.

"These two should be fine. They're still weeks away. This one here," Robert said, motioning his head toward the first cow, "I want her in the corral behind the house. We'll have to get her to the barn and load her into a trailer. She could drop this calf today."

Robert climbed onto Lucy just as the first snowflakes began to fall. He turned the troubled cow and started herding her back toward the ranch. "We're only a couple hundred yards from the fence," he yelled. "I've got this one. You get the other two and follow along."

Robert cursed at the pregnant cow, trying to coax her into motion. He spurred Lucy, started back for the ranch. The cow moved slowly at first, before picking up her feet faster as Lucy nearly tripped her from behind.

"Careful with her," Jack yelled as he turned the other two cows toward the ranch. In the distance, his friend wheeled in his saddle and fired a look that didn't need words. It wasn't Jack's ranch; they weren't Jack's cows. Jack wasn't going to lose a calf and the price of beef didn't matter to him when he wrote out his mortgage check.

The two rode toward the break and Robert continued herding quickly. His horse galloped out in front of the cow and waited for it to catch up. He rained down obscenities, trying to get her to move, his cheeks burning the color of his crimson ears. Spit flowed. Lucy whinnied. Snow started speckling the ground.

"Slow down, Robert." Jack rode carefully, keeping sight of his cows while steering Annie delicately across the hard ground. The snow fell faster. Visibility diminished with each flake.

Robert rounded back toward Jack. He came up alongside his friend, a scathing sneer evident through the white veil of winter. "I can't afford to lose a damn calf. You get these two back to the pen. I'm going to take her to the barn and double back to help you fix the break. Then we can get out of this damn weather."

Jack sunk in his saddle like a scolded child. He didn't say a word, just nodded.

The flask emerged from Robert's jacket. Another drink. He offered, but Jack shook his head. One more scornful look before Robert spurred Lucy again.

Robert galloped toward the ranch. Through the falling snow, he grew smaller as the distance between him and Jack increased. Jack could no longer see the pregnant cow stumbling toward the barn.

His nerves kicked. The ground beneath Annie was rougher than he imagined it would be that morning. A cracked hoof would mean months of care, and thousands of dollars spent on a part-time horse. He wished to be back in his heated basement in Helena, sitting in a leather recliner in front of the television. His wife never asked him why he needed a weekend escape from his family when he spent all of his time at work. Perhaps she understood that he was scared of what came next. Jack looked up and could barely trace the outline of his friend in the distance.

A yelp. Lucy fell. She kicked and scrambled on her side. Robert was beneath her. She tried to roll onto her legs and fell again. Robert dragged himself to the side. She rolled and kicked the air. Primitive screams.

Jack rode up and leapt from Annie. He ran to Robert, saw him kneeling on the ground, body unbroken. He looked at Lucy. Her right front leg had snapped just above the hoof.

"You all right?" Jack said. Wind grabbed his breath and carried his words away.

Robert pushed himself to his feet, coldness slid over his eyes. Jack walked in front of him.

"Robert?"

Robert said nothing. His gaze was fixed somewhere in the western distance, at the frozen ranch in front of him, or perhaps somewhere far beyond it.

"Robert? You okay?"

Silence. Robert's eyes slowly closed.

"God damn it," Robert's voice, low in a whisper. He ripped out his flask and took a long drink before capping it and throwing it against a fencepost. "Badger holes, god damn it."

The whisper grew to a roar, echoed through the valley. He walked to the fencepost and kicked it hard with his worn boot. "Fucking Seattle, Nathan. God damn it." Robert kicked the post again, panting as he tried to regain his breath.

He slumped down onto the ground, his back against the post. "Nathan, my son."

He buried his face into crossed forearms, his voice muffled by his canvas coat. "I can't keep doing it."

Jack remained quiet. He could have said he heard from the Carters that the price of beef would be better next fall. A better price and Robert could hire a hand like the Andersons always had. He could have pointed out that Stainbrook was buying the ranches at more than full value. Maybe say that everyone in the valley was impressed with Nathan's new job, that the other members of the Board genuinely cared for him. Or he could have mentioned his own problems with work in the city, his fear of getting older, of dying. He said none of these things. He only walked over to the fencepost, picked up the flask, and handed it to Robert.

"He's gone," Jack said. He sat down on the ground next to his friend, placed his hand on Robert's shoulder.

"I came home to run the ranch and that's what he should have done too."

"People like you, they're getting rarer. It's going to happen to the Andersons one day, and the Carters too, until all the family ranches die out. That's how this story ends."

"How bad is the break?" Robert said.

Lucy lay on her side, eyes open. Helpless whinnies escaped her mouth. From their spot near the fencepost, her massive back blocked sight of her foot.

"She's not going to be able to make it back."

Jack slowly unsheathed the knife clipped to his belt, a gift from his own son the previous Christmas. He opened it, and handed it to Robert. "She's suffering."

"Damn it, Jack, she was a good horse. I let Nathan name her. A curse."

"Can't blame the boy, Robert. It's not his fault."

Robert held the knife in his left hand, slowly turning the scaled handle in his palm. He let the hand fall to his side and slumped down further against the fence post. His eyes were closed, but his face was twisted in such a way that the sight made Jack's chest ache. A few feet away, Lucy lay motionless on the ground, no longer trying to stand. Jack put his arm around Robert. A small squeeze. Silent, they sat together.

Snowflakes began sticking to the hats and coats of the men slumped against the fence, to the back of Annie and the side of Lucy, all the way down to the break in her leg. Soon the flakes would grow larger and fall faster, and cover the entire ranch with a thick white blanket of snow, and everything would disappear beneath it, and 3,000 acres of family ranchland south of the Elkhorns would turn into an empty canvas.

The Confession of Fred Garrison at Tigers Crossing

Kevin Lee Peterson

I

The first time I seen Ben, he was walking up Picacho Pike from the direction of Tigers Crossing. Or, more like he was skipping, the rough-and-tumble way you might imagine a giant to skip, if he ever had a need to. I knew then he was a interesting fellow, as he was wearing a contraption on both of his feet, had a spring action and made him appear taller than he was. I also knew a interesting fellow was not a popular fellow in Tigers Crossing. Or, he was a popular fellow in a unpopular kind of way.

Later this same afternoon, as I was concerned the community would not be accepting to our new friend, I headed down to Larry's, ask if he run into the boy yet.

"Been through twice today," he tells me. He's hunched over a case of potato chips, crease ironed into his trousers.

"I suppose they're already talking about him at Duke's," I speculate.

Larry's eyes pelt me a second, and then he turns away. "People let each other be."

I give him a look so as to say, "You and I both know that ain't true," but then I ask him about the contraption the fellow wears on his feet.

"If you had to ask me," he tells me, slicing through packing tape with a blade, "I'd say it aids him to walk. He's crippled."

"The boy ain't a cripple!" I'm hot to say. Seeing as how I got a bad hip and walk with a limp, I'm sensitive to the word.

Larry faces me with a look I perceive condescending. He's tidy, holding the cardboard under his arm. Lot of folks can't read him as he ain't demonstrative, but I could always pick up a subtlety. Liked watching him fold into himself when he was annoyed.

I give room as Larry slides past to get rid of the cardboard he's carrying. "Y'all get any fresh milk this week," I yell after him. "Well, I'll have to pick me up a gallon this evening. I'm on my way to Duke's."

Now, Duke ain't the proprietor no more. His son took over ten, twelve years ago. Has a peculiar name most the folks can't pronounce, so pretty quick after he took over it got to be he was called Duke as well. After his pa died he accepted the title proud. Funny thing is, at the funeral - which was five, six years ago - we all learned Duke wasn't his pa's name neither. Anyway, I go up there a afternoon for a beer. Thins the blood a little.

What I expect at Duke's is a empty bar except for Squirrels holding down one end, off his shift at the factory. He's what I call a hard-nosed fellow, and he'd have to be, considering all Tigers Crossing knows his wife is seeing Larry on the sly. Requires a hard nose just to face the plain of day.

"How we doing today, Duke?" I take my place at the bar.

"Mr. Garrison." Duke welcomes me by popping the top off a beer bottle, and then he returns to a conversation with his other patron.

Raising my beer, I sit back casual, so as to listen in on Squirrels and Duke. Thing is, I'm a little hard of hearing and even though the music ain't blaring, it muffles the voices so I can't make out what they're saying.

"Ah, so you seen the newcomer," I say. "I thought y'all might be talking about him over here."

"We ain't talking about nobody, Fred." Squirrels is defensive.

Duke raises himself straight, though, signaling to me he seen the boy. "He was here. Strange fellow. About noon he ordered a beer, standing right where you're sitting, except he was bouncing from foot to foot, like he couldn't keep still."

"Larry says he's a cripple."

Duke considers the information, but then he tells me, "I don't know about that. I think he's got a condition. He asked if he could take his beer outside, to which I informed him it was against the law. So he took his beer here and paced the length of the bar with it, not so much walking as bounding back and forth." He wipes down the counter, allowing the scene he's drawn to fill out. "Since there was no one else here, I told him, sure, you can go outside. So he took his beer outside and did laps around the establishment. I saw him once every 30 seconds or so, bouncing past the window here. Like I said, I think he's got a condition."

I want to talk more, but I decide to take my exit, as the entire shift from the factory is filing in, and I was practically their boss before I retired.

At this time, as there ain't a police force in Tigers Crossing, and the only patrolling we get is for special calls, aside from the weekly drive through by Deputy Dave, I feel a sense of duty to make a sweep of the place once, twice a day, just to see everything's OK and nobody needs assistance.

So I take the Pike up past the old school, circle the church, and come back down toward the Crossing. Cars are packed like sardines into Duke's lot, signaling to me it's opportune occasion to make a pass through the trailer park.

Some of the boys don't take good care their woman and children down there, and about this time the wives get to feeling anxious their husbands might come home with some kinda agenda. It comforts the women to see someone is looking out for them, and they're more prone to be forthright with their grievances when they fear a scene is brewing.

The trailer park is typically quiet this time of day, which it is. Being so hot in the afternoon most the women and children lock themselves up in the air conditioning. The husbands bring the party back in the cool of the evening, and everyone come outside, little kids running every which way while the men drink and the women sit quiet and tense.

I can feel the anticipation of the drunken men, and I pull in easy next to Squirrels' place.

Now, I always got two things on my mind, like in addition to the thoughts run through my head, I got a internal ear listening in on what my heart and my guts got to say. People think it's a clairvoyance how I can tell a thing will happen before it goes down, but I look at it more scientific. It's a matter of experience and paying attention. It's not so much a sixth sense as a working together of the five, and their communication isn't the articulation of words but a feeling.

I'm vibrating with the engine, in front of Squirrels' place, when a rock come whizzing past my good ear and dings off my truck. At first I'm thinking it's kids playing ambush, but then I see it's Squirrels' wife doing the throwing, and she's aiming to let another one launch.

Woman is standing a force to be reckoned with, and I ain't too slow to pick up the message she's sending my way. Or, maybe I ain't quick enough to avoid taking it square off the forehead. Anyhow, when there's trouble planted deep in a person, it can show thorns at the slightest irritation, nicking a passerby just for being too near, so I don't take it too personal. Looking back, after gaining a great enough distance, I kind of admire her defiance. And her little dress.

The funny thing about all the looking out I been doing for our new friend is, he's the one come and find me. By the time I get back from my rounds, he's having a laugh with Pete - my friend I rent the property - and the two of them are talking kind of sly while they walk the perimeter.

I was hoping to mitigate introductions between these two, seeing as how Pete can be a little off-putting to unconditioned ears. When I find the two of them together I'm feeling worried he might scare off our new friend, but I'm also contended, seeing the duty is relieved me. So I pull up in front of my homestead, across a empty lot from Pete's studio, and brew my afternoon coffee, which I take as a pick-me-up right about this time.

"Boy, sure is a hot one today," I holler, so as to be cordial.

They nod in my direction, and I sip my coffee, enjoying the dry heat and looking forward to the sunset.

While I'm sitting out front a car turns off the highway, and I recognize pretty quick it's Mary, who come once, twice a week to sit and relieve her grievances.

Mary ain't my wife, as I ain't such a conventional man, but she's more a friend whose company I don't mind sharing every so often. Works at the Wal-Mart with Pete, and also has a wild idea or two brewing in her noggin, except her deviances and Pete's ain't ever in harmony. They agree the country's gone to waste and the government can't be trusted, but after this point - and I ain't a scholar on deviants – their ideologies clash like hot soup and coleslaw.

Mary and I get some wieners sizzling, pop open a beer. I can tell we got our new friend's attention, and eventually he and Pete come pay us a visit.

I have a good spotlight on my front porch and Pete walks into it, slouching some. Ben sticks to the perimeter of the beam so I can't make him out too good, but sure enough he's bounding from foot to foot and the contraption on his feet is launching him like a trampoline.

"Pete, I do believe this marks the first occasion I have the honor of meeting one of your friends," I say, making light of his mood.

"Well Ben, what brings you to our humble community? Why don't you step onto the porch here, we can get a look at you?"

When I do finally see the boy face to face I can tell right away how Larry might of mistook him a cripple. He steps into the light a moment, and I see his body is mangled, like a lumberjack wrung through a runaway pile of timber. His skin is leather and his bones protrude to a point they'd pierce softer hide. Thing strikes me most powerful is, the sinister grimace he's wearing, a smile eating up his entire face.

I'm not one to hold a person to first impressions, as there's more to a man than meets the eye, so I make a point to talk to Ben normal, even though he's about the most unnormal thing I ever seen. But I'm also aware he's aware he ain't normal, and I don't want to give him the injustice of pretending I can't see him. So I offer him a beer and then, very diplomatic, give a nod to his condition without presenting the impression it makes me uncomfortable.

"Sounds like you could use some grease," I say to him. He erupts in a hearty laugh, twisted though it is, breaks the ice right before our eyes.

Ben steps into the shadow with a beer and Mary and Pete and I start talking as we do, show our guest his presence ain't a affectation to our gathering. Of course it is anyhow, and Mary and Pete are extra polite to one another.

"What kind of crazy things you read on your computer today?" I say to Pete. "Pete's quiet at first, but once you get him going, he won't shy away from telling you the thoughts in your head aren't those of your own."

Since he ain't game, I turn to Mary, ask her to share what's new in her world.

She clings to me a little, but I can tell she's excited to tell us something, see what the newcomer makes of it.

"Mercury is in retrograde," she tells us. Then with some drama, "My receptors have been confused all week."

Any other night Pete would of scoffed at such a remark. Instead he turns, looks to Ben.

"Well, Ben. You know Mercury is in retrograde?" I ask him.

"Hadn't felt it," he tells us, smile screeching to his ears.

We sit silent a time, hush weighing heavy on our shoulders. The contraption on Ben's feet is rhythmic, tinny as a drip.

In such a situation I like to remove myself from the present and witness the scene from outside. Offers me perspective and takes the pressure off. Instead of reaching for the next thing to say, I'm regarding the crowd, observing the nervous tick plays with Pete's hands, the deep breaths Mary has prescribed herself. I get to thinking about Lizzie, and I feel a longing to reconcile with her, tell her I'm on her side. Even if she is committing sin, she's still in a position probably makes her miserable 99% of the time. I see she don't want my help, though. Didn't ask for it.

I look at Pete and it depresses me he don't got the gumption to go out, get a girl. His skin is milk like Lizzie's, except he don't take good care his hygiene. He's licking his chapped lips and I can see the gears grinding behind the twitch in his eye. It's good he come over for real company instead of spending all day on his computer, but it still bothers me he wastes so much time and energy getting caught up in conspiracy don't concern him. He is a young man, I have to remind myself.

"What's the soft patch growing there above your lip?" I tease.

Mary reacts by squeezing my arm and adjusting her seat, like she just come to from a trance. I turn my attention in her direction as she crosses her legs and smooths over her dress. Mary has these little gestures, shows she's in control of her person. I see how it might poke Pete pretty raw, as he thinks we ain't got no control at all. I like her demeanor, though, slipping away from all proximity then regaining herself, serious and proper.

Breaking the silence Ben states, "I'm going to stretch out my legs," and just like that he's off doing laps around the property.

Before the rest of us unwind, I take the opportunity and turn to Pete. "What were you and your new friend talking over so long while I was sipping my coffee?" I ask him.

"Nothing," Pete tells me.

"Oh come on, Pete, y'all were at it nearly two hours."

"It ain't your business, Fred."

So we sit a while longer, surrounded by the sound of Ben stretching his legs, until Pete tells us he's going home, got a early shift tomorrow.

Mary and I share one another's warmth a time, as it cools off quick at the Crossing, even after a hot day. Then she heads off, too.

To my surprise, as our new friend hasn't said more than two words to me, he come back to the porch and asks for another beer.

"Your name is Fred Garrison," he tells me.

"Yes it is," I say, intrigued at where he's headed.

"Where were you born?" His way of speaking is direct, but I can't read his intentions, which I'm usually sensitive to.

"I was born right here, at Tigers Crossing," I say, drawing out his hand.

"And your parents. Where were they born?"

Now I'm regarding our new friend fairly hard. I don't mind the interview, but I don't have a notion where he's coming from. I talked to cripples who speak real direct, like a overcompensation, but the jagged smile on Ben's face lace his words wry, like he's on the verge of telling a joke.

I take a sip of my beer and cross my legs. "My ma is from coal mining country and my pa is from the plains," I say to him, but I'm cautious he's taking me for a ride.

Ben ruminates the information. Then he asks me, "Many of the people here, did you grow up with them?"

"No," I say. "Most the people here come from some other place where they worked some other factory job. That's why my pa come here. For work." I stop a moment, but he's expecting more. "Back when I was in grade school, the place up the Pike was kindergarten through seniors. Now the students take a bus to Arlington every morning and join the city kids. No, the way I say it, all my friends are either dead or MIA. Married In Arlington.

"We had a good football team back in my day. I was recruited, you know, played two seasons at A&M before I broke my hip. When I come home after sophomore year I took a job at the factory, but I couldn't do manual labor, so they stuck me in the office. Never went back to school. Realized then the bubble I was living under. My friends at the college were excited where their life was going, but from outside it appeared fantasy, like they were fulfilling a prophecy. After graduation they all moved to the city and started a family, making solid the future they were so eager to get to. I had a sweetheart before I dropped out, been dating since the 10th grade. Guess where she's at."

But Ben changes direction. Tells me, "I have a proposition for you."

I'm taken aback, but I say to him, "Shoot."

The smile on his face is crawled all the way ear to ear, and his skin is cracked and wrinkled. "I'm willing to pay you," he starts telling me. Then he goes on to explain he can't keep still long enough to read. It's his lot to stay on the move, travel from town to town. "During my next journey," he tells me, "I would like to listen to your voice reading a book."

Ben lets what he's said hang in the air, and we both take a sip of our beer. I'm thinking I appreciate how direct he come and state his plight.

I ask him, "What's the proposition?"

"I have a tape recorder in my backpack," and I see for the first time he's got a bag tied tight against his body, like a extension to his back.

The proposition he delivers is step-by-step instruction how he wants me to read a book all the way through, then read each chapter individual a second time before I ever hit record. Tells me he's had other clients struggle behind the microphone and this is the system he come up with to find their voice. Takes practice to "act like yourself," he tells me.

I lean in like I'm real interested in the business end of the transaction. "How much you paying for such a service?" I ask him, curious of the price he put on such a odd assignment.

"$10 an hour," he tells me, and says he would trust me to log my hours honest. On top of the hourly wages he would even throw in a $100 bonus if I finished the project in two weeks' time.

As I ain't one to turn down a interesting endeavor, I sit back to consider what it all might entail. After letting him hang a minute I announce, "On one condition. You got to tell me who you are. What's the contraption on your feet?"

"My story takes a long time to tell," he tells me. Then he goes on to explain there are muscles in the human body function involuntary, but in his case he has to pump one manual. He tells me, "This is my heartbeat."

II

Ben leaves me the book and the recording device, in addition to written instruction in the hand of a boy just learning to copy the alphabet. He also leaves me the weight of responsibility, and under its pressure I perceive a change in my demeanor. Those about the Crossing interpret my mood somber, like a gray cloud is following my movements, hanging low over mind and spirit. It ain't a cloud, though, so much as a mirror, and in its reflection I see myself and through myself I see the people and things about me. It's a time of introspection for me, as I'm preparing to perform the task at hand. I'm walking with a gravity 'cause I was allowed a insight, singled out, privy to a man's plight.

I'm taking Ben's instruction serious, and it's why I don't start reading the book right away. I want to warm up to the assignment, feel the weight of its importance. I carry the book on my mind and with it a level head, express myself contemplative.

I walk the aisles at Larry's, seeing what's on the shelf. What it's there for, who's buying it. With the extra spending money I'd be collecting, I could afford to treat myself, a necessity during my heightened sense of awareness.

"Ben come and see me," I say to Larry. "Let me in on who he is."

He's busy sweeping the floor.

"Our new friend," I say, recognizing Larry don't even know his name. "He's a intellectual. Receives his learning by unconventional means, and asked for my help. I reckon he's a long way from home," I say. "No, he ain't a cripple, but he does have a condition, keeps him on the go." I fill Larry in on the job Ben has for me.

"Ought to keep you busy," is all Larry has to say, reaching for a dust bunny under the shelf.

A factory worker walks in for a pack of cigarettes, and Larry meets him at the register.

"Anyway, Ben sought me out last night. He's on a expedition to see this part of the country. Probably how hard the ground is suits him, as he's got to create some pressure, keep his heart going." I pause to see if what I'm saying is pinching Larry peculiar. "Did he tell you about his condition?"

"Didn't mention it." Larry is slighting me, about to pick up his broom.

"You're so cold you must be a devil," I chuckle. But then I appeal to his sense of business. "Tell me, Lar," I say. "I got a extra dollar needs spending. What's your fanciest chocolate?"

Now I have his attention as he sets down the broom and returns to the register. Larry don't say nothing but slides a bar shaped like a pyramid onto the counter.

"Ring me up for one," I say to him.

At Duke's I follow suit under the same mentality, order a draft beer instead of the regular bottle. The boys can't account for the change, and I'm in no hurry to shed light.

I sip my beer thoughtful and take a load off, reaching a equilibrium with my surroundings. Duke and Squirrels are talking on the sly again, but I don't interrupt, nor do I try and listen in. More like, I'm feeling out the state of things between them.

They ain't minding me a nickel, tells me I ain't their topic of discussion. Far as I can make out Squirrels is doing most the talking, but his demeanor is collected and not the usual barrage of complaints and insults.

I'm keeping my eyes open, but my mind wanders off. I'm thinking about Lizzie, and how she ever come to marry a guy like Squirrels in the first place. Maybe it was she's new in town and he's got a steady job, even if he's only the janitor. Girl must of been in desperate straights to marry a little rascal such as Squirrels. Once she had a chance to settle down and find some comfort, she realized her position. Love and support can be mistaken for one another, but the words ain't synonyms. Standing on her own two feet, Lizzie towered over Squirrels. May of took some time to get there, but once she arrived she couldn't help but see broader horizons.

"Another draft, Mr. Garrison?" I'm nearly finished with my pint when Duke strolls down the bar.

"Got to keep a clear head," I say. "I'm on assignment. Our friend Ben stop by last night and inquired for my assistance." I see from the corner of my eye Squirrels is intrigued. "Young man is of the world. Sure, he's got a condition, but he's a intellectual of some renown. You talk to the boy, yet?"

"It ain't a condition," Squirrels hisses under his breath.

"A condition so rare it ain't got a name," I correct. "If you can get past it, you might find it helpful to talk to him, get a outsider's point of view. He talked to Pete yesterday and I could tell immediate the conversation had effect on him. Poor guy was

spooked someone come and tell him straight about all his conspiracy beliefs. Anyhow, it ain't everyday we get a famous intellectual
around these parts, have the opportunity to pick his brain. Maybe
he'd have advice for your woman problem."

Instead of lashing out at me, Squirrels stares hard into his
glass. Gives me a chill.

I turn to my own beer. Taking the rest down in one gulp I
state, "I do like a beer a afternoon." And it's the truth.

Feeling receptive to the Crossing and of clear and articulate
mind, I make a pass through the trailer park, just to see I don't
pick up some vibration I hadn't felt under previous conditions. I
don't stop in front of Lizzie's but pull through on a roll.

The next morning Ben intercepts me as I'm pulling out
the drive.

"Grab your five-gallon gasoline can and meet me at Larry's,"
he tells me, then run down the road.

When I show up he's waiting at the pump, hopping from
foot to foot. "You grab your fuel, and I'll grab mine." A minute
later he drops a gallon of water and a sack of provisions onto the
passenger seat.

I'm getting the inclination he's wanting to go somewhere, but
I ain't exactly sure how it's gonna work. Before I know it, though,
he's leaping north out of town and moving at a good clip, and I'm
nearly breaking the speed limit just to keep pace with him.

The boy appears loose and it occurs to me he's in a more natural state. We're moving 35, 40 miles an hour, and my truck is working harder than he is. His smile ain't so crooked, kind of pulled even
by the sheer force of speed, takes the furrow right out of his brow.

"Well," I yell out the window. "I got about 30 gallons of gasoline and all day in front of me. Ample time to tell me who you are?"

Ben twists his smile a minute, and shifts into a higher gear.
The smell of hot metal is wafting off his contraption into the
cabin of my truck.

Maybe we're two hours north of the Crossing when Ben signals to follow him off-road to a oak tree stands alone next to the highway. Once I come to a stop he grabs the provisions out from the passenger-side window and proceeds to pour half the gallon of water down his throat in one draft. He hands the jug to me then starts snacking on beef jerky and trail mix.

I see the destination is calculated as I got just enough gas, including the can I filled, to get me back home. I refuel while Ben is taking a leak in the adjacent field, a sight to see, as he hops from foot to foot.

Under the oak tree Ben asks me for the time.

"About noon," I say.

"Don't look up," he admonishes. "You're facing due east. It's noon and we're one month shy of the autumnal equinox. Close your eyes and point out the sun."

I consider his instruction a minute, thinking the sun is at its highest point in the sky at noon, but I ain't sure where that is. "I'd just be guessing," I admit. "What's this all about?"

"Tell me, does the earth revolve around the sun, or does the sun revolve around the earth? You can open your eyes."

I think he's pulling my leg, so I look him over, suspicious. "Earth revolves around the sun," I say.

"Good. And where does the sun rise in the morning? And where does it set at night?"

"Rises in the east and sets in the west."

"Good. And how do you know that?"

"Well, it occurs everyday," I state, confounded by the expedition.

"Sure enough. Where then, pray tell, did the sun rise this morning?" The humor on his face is coy.

At this time I'm near exhausted by his game, and I let it be known by heaving a sigh. "Sun rises in the east," I point. "But it only rises due east once a year, if I recall."

"You recall!" He laughs and claps his hands. "You know the sun rises in the east, and you know it rises (not once, but) twice a year due east, because someone taught you that it is so. Have you ever considered that you wouldn't have any reason to believe that the earth revolves around the sun except that someone taught you it is so as well? And yet it's ridiculous to think it could be otherwise; that someone could have ever believed otherwise."

I'm tired of what Ben's saying, but he turns serious.

"It's merely information," he tells me, grabbing my wrist with his leathery hand. "Without understanding the physics behind the phenomenon, it's merely information. And people believe in it religiously."

I look up through the leaves of the oak we're standing under, at the sun prickling through, and I can feel what Ben is talking about.

"Reminds me, what you're telling me, of Pete and all the time he spends on the computer looking up conspiracy. He's a smart cookie, knows a lot of information like you're saying, but in another regard it's like it ain't his own life. Or, it is his own life 'cause it's all he makes of it.

"I like the company of someone like Pete or Mary 'cause they think different, but it's like they're stuck in their own little world and can't see what's all around them. Can't feel the sun the same way you and I are feeling it right this moment."

"Each validates his experience," Ben tells me. He don't offer any more, and I'm thinking, I also like the company of Ben, as he makes me think.

Ben departs on the outskirts of town after waving goodbye, flashes his smile one more time, and I drive the rest of the way alone in the evening sun.

Quite a few cars parked at Duke's, but the place ain't rocking, as if there's a séance inside. When I pull in my drive I can see Pete and Mary are waiting for me.

"Squirrels attacked Larry today," Pete blurts out, and the body language between he and Mary tells me they been sitting out some time, tension rising and ebbing.

Pete's tied in a knot, strain on his hands, when he tells me, "One of the factory workers happened by, broke up the scene. Larry called in the deputy."

"Ah, well Deputy Dave come to the rescue. No need to worry," I try and lift the mood.

Mary is sitting back, so calm she's stiff. She elaborates, "Larry's asked for a restraining order, and he'll get it. Squirrels was carrying a gun, Fred."

But Pete interrupts, unable to contain himself. "There's something else," he says. "I looked up Ben online, to see if anyone wrote about him."

Then Pete tells me a guy in Bisbee, AZ has a theory, calls Ben a manipulator. Ben left Bisbee in a uproar, but he couldn't put his finger on why, exactly. It wasn't he committed a crime, but more like he was involved from the outside, pulling strings. So this fellow traveled to nearby towns, see if Ben was getting around. Turns out he was seen all over the county, and everyone he met reported a sort of disruption or uneasy feeling he left.

"I have been picking up strange vibrations ever since Ben arrived," Mary chimes in. "At first I attributed them to Mercury being in retrograde, but I think it's Ben who brought them here."

"We don't know this guy," Pete pleads to me. "He come to town a complete stranger, and we took interest in him for being unique."

The blast of thunder wakes me around midnight. "I knew it's coming," I'm saying to myself. Lightning is putting on a show, causing a shadow to dance. It takes a minute to realize power is down.

I feel sick when I remember Ben out there, soaked through. I see him in my mind, seeking shelter under a tree, but then I know he can't stand on wet ground.

Lightning flashes, enforces a sense of remoteness, like I'm the one is trapped.

"I ain't helpless," I say, and I dress quick to go out and find Ben.

Thing is, I don't have to look far. I'm hardly out the door when he come hobbling down the drive, lame. I set him up on the porch so he can beat his heart against the side of the house.

Finally I see how grave it is. He's twisted his ankle bad, can't put weight on it. Each pump is agony.

"Got to take the contraption off," I say, and he don't react for the pain he's in will intensify.

He pumps and I pull up his pant leg. I'm wanting for a flashlight, but I can't leave his side. Then I see the buckle in a lightning flash. He pumps and I undo the contraption. He pumps and I loosen it best I can.

"I'm gonna yank this thing off, and it's gonna hurt like hell," I say to him. I can tell he's bracing himself, though he still don't talk.

He pumps one more time and I give a strong pull against the recoil as to be sure and remove the thing in one movement.

His foot is hideous and his ankle looks even worse.

I have scraps of wood and metal laying around the property so I gather a two-by-four and place it against the house, give him a even and solid surface, then I go searching for something I can use to brace his ankle. I come back with two pieces of PVC Pipe and run inside for duct tape.

Ben can put any weight on his ankle at all tells me it ain't broken, though it's swelled up black and blue like a bloated turkey neck.

"The pressure I'm about to apply ain't gonna feel good, but it'll guide and support," I say to him. Then I tape the two pieces of PVC on either side of his ankle, which ain't easy to do as he's pumping both of his feet against the wall. When I feel it's secure I grab him ibuprofen and ice, help with the swelling. He's a tough kid. He's in pain, but the fear of death is washed off his face.

The lightning lets up but it's still raining steady a hour later, and I suggest we take off the contraption on his other foot as well. "At least let's get your feet clean," I say, making light of the situation. Ben's got a sense of humor, and he return a weak laugh.

I look at the nails wrapped around the front of each toe and says, "It's a while since you took it off?" Then I bring the contraption into the house, place it upside down on the radiator so as to dry out the smell in addition to the fabric inside, but I remember the power is out.

III

We were up most the night and I can state confident Ben opened more to me than he ever did to anyone before. It's not I pressed him, just he was grateful to have a friend. The pain subsiding he reached a mixed state of fatigue and optimism in his convalescence, melted him. When he talked the words come off the top his head, listless maybe except they were sincere. It was nice to converse without the pretense.

I was tired too and I don't remember what he was saying exactly, but it ain't real important. It was more a brotherly bond we shared. Once I wrapped his leg the best I could and clipped his toenails for him - no easy task I might add - we moved in from the rain and settled the night in my little abode.

Mostly we sat and listened to the weather. We appreciated the silence between our ears and the patter all around. Ben's heartbeat was muted, since he wasn't wearing his contraption.

Feeling chummy I asked him, "You ever make love to a woman?"

He looked to me sheepish. His smile revealing a innocence.

"It's the best thing in this world. Not the love making, but the contact. Touching another person. Holding her." Ben glanced at his feet, and I got the picture I was rubbing him the wrong way.

"Someone would love to be your woman," I tried to comfort him. "Imagine the thrill she'd get touching your heart, pumping your heart to give you life. If you sought it, you would find it. Maybe you ain't fated to the road. Sure you got to keep a move on, but you could alter your direction a little, run circles around a tighter center. You'd fit right in."

I could tell he appreciated the gesture, but it was a fantasy wouldn't come true. So we sat silent again. I observed the boy was exhausted, a tired no sleep could unwind, and I realized then he was only a child.

"Are you having a good run?" I asked him, and he flashed his smile at me. "Where will you go from here?"

I must of dozed off.

I woke late in my easy chair, and Ben was gone. Only thing he left behind's the book he gave me, laying right where it laid all week. Since he took his recording device, I knew he wasn't coming back.

I sat in my chair some time, content in the morning stupor, replaying last night in my head. I touched a soft spot on the rascal, I know. Maybe it was the closest he'd been to a person since leaving his hometown, but I understood he wasn't gonna stay.

"Each validates his experience," Ben told me. He didn't talk much, but what he did say stuck like flies to a horse. Then I got to thinking about Pete and Mary, how they turned on Ben so fast, nearly turned me against him, too.

I was gonna miss Ben. There'd be a hole in my conversations with Pete and Mary, like Ben revealed to me they were both holding jokers under the layers conspired around them. I wanted to relate to them the events took place, but at the same time I didn't want to speak with them at all, like I wanted to keep Ben to myself.

"It is a disruption," I said out loud. But it wasn't exactly a negative thing, so long as one could handle it, the insight.

I brewed a coffee and took it on the porch, felt a unreal distance between the previous night and where I was at. The ground was rich brown and pools of water stood where it depressed.

I heard a siren in the distance, at the Crossing. Then I heard another. I took my time 'cause I knew it was all over. When I pulled up to Larry's, Deputy Dave was standing next to his cruiser, amid a fury of lights. Everyone kind of hovered about, like they were unsure how to proceed.

When I seen the body bag I didn't need ask who it was. It was fitting he was folded up so neat, like cardboard taken out to the recycling.

"Deputy Dave," I nodded to the young man.

He looked at me stiff, but I could tell there was a earthquake rumbling under his uniform. I hung around a minute, but there was nothing for me to do.

About noon I made a pass through the trailer park. From outside I sensed the grief and anger confused Lizzie's home, even though it was quiet. I determined to help her when the time was right, offer her whatever condolence was in my power.

On my way home I chanced to see the shadow of my truck crawling through the Crossing, stealthy, like it was fixing to pounce on some invisible prey. In my living room I picked up the book Ben left me. There was a messaged inscribed on the first page.

"Thanks, Fred. I know it was a lot to ask of you."

Fullness

Amanda Marbais

"Come on, bitch. Get in the car," said Muriel. Muriel and Julie, adorned with green eye shadow, glitter peppering their domed hair, picked me up in a battered Subaru. Julie cranked the stereo, blasting the Stone Temple Pilots. My father looked out the window and turned on the floodlights in warning.

We drove to the high school and drank Southern Comfort from Dairy Queen cups in the parking lot. Staring out our windshields, we talked about the school bullshit we didn't understand. Someone had burned FUCK HIGH SCHO into the hillside with acid from the chem lab, but got caught before he finished.

My own family had moved twelve times, so I was always new. My popularity never seemed to gain traction. That night I passed from one person's car to the next, drank too much, blacked out and ended up in a Pacer, at Red Head, with Peggy Meyer, holding a blunt. Peggy, eyes red, caked with septic-looking eye-shadow, cried about some sack-of-shit boyfriend who didn't care she had been sexually assaulted at a party in the ninth grade. She couldn't shut up about that party. Her mascara was running.

"That sucks so bad, Peggy. That sucks so bad," I said.

"It's okay, Mary. You don't even know me."

She started the car, using my name over and over again, like an incantation, asking me please not to tell.

"I probably won't remember," I said.

In a miniscule town, people spilled their secrets to the out-sider. I guess no one wanted to shit in their own camp.

I got this job at a tourist trap, Captain Black's Sweet Shop, to be away from home. I was always trying to get in with other families. It annoyed some mothers, but others ate it up. Occasionally, these mothers treated me like a temporary daughter, and it worked out, a safe-harbor where I could fill up between moves. I had hung out at Muriel's house a hundred times before Homecoming, often staying overnight on the weekends, my small duffle bag in the corner of their laundry room, my temporary shelter. I also kept a duffle in my car to hedge my bets.

Muriel had an abortion our junior year. She was the only girl I knew to get an abortion. As my best friend, she spent fall semester crying in my Rabbit. She told me, under penalty of death, not to repeat it. I swore on my little sister, the only family member I liked.

In Captain Black's shitty basement, Julie and I put our full weight on the freezer to tamp the chicken that arrived from Sysco. We jumped on the freezer like wrestlers, ignoring the possibility of rupturing the plastic bags, spraying chicken-fat over storage shelves.

"I'm done with this. Let's put the pickle bucket on it."

Julie lit a cigarette and sipped her Styrofoam cup filled with Coke and JD. "Don't tell anyone I made out with Kim."

"'kay."

"Do you think I'm gross, because we went down on each other?"

"No."

"Don't fucking tell anyone."

Upstairs, Muriel had turned up the radio and the register drawer dinged open. She'd locked the front doors. "I didn't think you guys were going to come back up. Count these." She threw a bag of change and it hit me in the chest. It wasn't cool, but I counted. Muriel could get away with a lot.

Julie, ever the pastor's kid, glinting with nose-rings and ironic '60s hair, piled high, ashed in a sundae bowl and fought tears.

Just then our coworker Crystal threw her tip-apron on the waitress station and said, "I need a beer and some fucking Santana." Crystal was whip-thin, tinged from spray tan, her shoulders rolled in to minimize her height. She turned to Julie. "What's wrong?" Julie just said, "Shut the fuck up, Crystal." Like most, Julie wore secrets badly, the bags under her eyes, the fearful, rabbity looks.

In the car, Muriel, Julie and I split a skunky joint Crystal gave us. She'd wanted to come. They made me be the asshole and say "no". She asked me to do something Sunday. I said no to that too.

We drove to Sparkle for cigs. We called Dax to get beer and waited a half hour, windows down, feet propped on car doors, pot and wood smoke making us dreamy. I felt I was visiting, before moving someplace real. I watched the ghostly patterns of swinging power-lines crisscross the blacktop. The traffic's taillights made disappearing comets around the bend, reaffirming freedom with a riptide of color.

"No responsibility to shoulder someone else's standards," I said.

"What are you talking about, Mary?" said Julie. She turned halfway around in the passenger's seat and gave me a shit-look.

Muriel interrupted her. "Bolton's sick," she said.

"So? Is he dead?" said Julie. She lit a cigarette.

"No. My mom took care of him."

"So?"

"He's my sister's kid."

"She should eat that shit up. She's a grandma." Julie toked off her cigarette. "They live for that."

"Not if you've raised two daughters. Seriously, she deserves a life," said Muriel. "She tried to make us all get IUDs. Bet she wishes that worked."

"She can't force you to get an IUD," said Julie.

"Yeah she can," said Muriel. "She should have."

In their friend's bedroom, Julie, Muriel, me, and five guys listened to the Dead Milkmen while drinking Peppermint

Schnapps from Muppets glasses on a race-car bed. There were Alyssa Milano posters everywhere. Perhaps it was an Ohio thing. What did I know? I was from Illinois. I felt like a voyeur peering in the window, above it, inside it.

"Your hair is cool." This guy named Stewart had Morrissey hair. He wore an Eraserhead T-shirt.

"It's not. I got it done at Family Clips," I said.

"Cool."

"It's actually not cool."

"Want to go outside and smoke?" he asked.

His 14-year-old sister was eating a sandwich, feet on the kitchen counter, in front of a 10-inch TV, watching *Beverly Hills, 90210* with a bemused and incendiary look. Stewart ruffled her bobbed hair.

On the porch, bracketed between two trellises of Morning Glories he said, "My mom has lung cancer. She got silicone breast implants. One busted and seeped into her lungs."

I touched my own breast. Could that happen?

"Don't tell anyone," he said.

"Uh," It was a grunt, like I'd been hit. I wrapped my arms around myself.

"I probably shouldn't have said anything."

He tried to kiss me. I didn't want him to touch my breast. I pressed my back into the trellis.

Two months later, Crystal and Muriel lounged in my Rabbit on break. Crystal tagged along because she was within earshot when we talked about smoking. In a parking space by the dumpster, we watched for the manager and listened to Bikini Kill. I was nearly a part of Muriel's family. I knew everything about them, and they even called me Little M. The car was filled with smoke and my favorite song screeching *I chewed on your sores.*

"Guys, I think I had a miscarriage," said Crystal.

"What the fuck are you talking about?" said Muriel.

"I was in the bathroom last night. It was like real bloody and chunky and shit."

"Are you okay now?" I said. I acted like she would bleed in front of us.

She pushed on her stomach. "I feel so full. Uh." She got out of the car to pee.

"Jesus," I said. We watched her walk to Captain Black's.

"God. She's such a slut," said Muriel. "Want to go to a party tonight?"

"No," I said, more aggressively than I meant it. I sounded like a real bitch.

I was over at Stewart's, wedging myself into their family, too. We had chicken, mashed potatoes, lemonade – what Stewart called "the works." The week prior, my dad drove into a tree on purpose. He had been driving my sister to track practice when he hit a massive oak in front of the country club. My sister wore a pink neck brace, which she complained of constantly, her head stiff and her eyes sunken in her face.

A few days after the accident, I felt compelled to unload this at school, and walked into several classrooms intending to corner my teacher with "Wait. Can I talk to you about…" But, other students always wandered into class, and I had the sense my teachers were too exhausted by life to care. I didn't blame them but I was beginning to feel like one of those ticks we found on my dog last summer, a grape with legs, crammed with everyone's sorrow. Even if I could, were these people worth telling? I hoped if I wore a neck brace someone from my adopted families might help me out. Then I remembered they had their own unspoken problems. I tried not to think about Stewart's Mom's cancer. I looked at her breasts.

After a while, it seemed absurd to make small talk. I excused myself to the Stewart's bathroom, and just hung out in the silence with the dog wallpaper and the matching orange towels, and the perfectly white ceramic floor. I was in there too long. Stewart's sister opened the door, came in, and closed the door quickly.

"Hey, how's it going?" I said. I was still on the toilet.

"I have to check my vag."

I didn't know what to say. "Okay."

"Oh. It itches so bad." She shoved her hands down her pants. "I've got crabs. I'm going to have to take a shower."

"Here. Let me get out of your way."

She'd turned on the water and was pulling down her pants. "I have pubic lice shampoo. It's real easy."

"Oh that's good." I didn't know why, but I still washed my hands while she was itching and cursing.

"Don't tell anyone at school."

"I'm telling everyone," I said.

"Stop being a smart-ass." She'd jumped in the shower and was lathering herself with the curtain open. "Bye," she said. She closed the curtain.

I went downstairs. Stewart was on the couch. He'd started *The Godfather* and he patted the couch cushion. I sat down like a zombie, and he didn't notice.

"Is it possible to know too much?" I said. Soon, I would get into the car and keep driving. It seemed totally possible. I had The Bag as I came to think of it, a duffle of deodorant, jeans, my New Order t-shirt, five hundred dollars, my brother's .22, some Carmex and bubble bath. Somehow it seemed like the right combination of provisions. I planned to leave everything, all the shit, right here.

"If you mean gossip, I wouldn't like you anymore if you spilled it about Mom. You got to keep that shit secret."

"Do you think your family would adopt me?" I said.

"No."

"Why?"

"Cause. Like, what if I stopped liking you?"

"Good point," I said.

"Not that it's going to happen." He squeezed my shoulder. "Sure."

The shooting started up in the *The Godfather*, sprays of bullets hitting Don Corleone. Even in those seconds you knew the family wouldn't be the same. You understood what it was like to realize yourself, to recognize you were transitioning without danger of interference, to go with the current, to become something new, reborn.

After a bad night, I casually told my parents to fuck off while they were watching Matlock. I said it like I was saying good-bye, but I was goose-pimpled, nauseated. Even in the blue TV light, you could see the shock register on their faces. I walked up the split-level stairs and out of the house. I revved my car's motor and cranked Pearl Jam. It was ridiculous. Eddie Vedder was screaming as I hit their mailbox and drove off. I needed some melodrama.

I would stay with Muriel for a couple days to collect my paycheck at work. I wouldn't tell her I was leaving. Why did she need to know? One more secret. I checked The Bag in my car – clothes, gun, Carmex. I thought of the Latin Club Award, the honor roll letter, the high school shit I left in a pile of Arby's trash by my bedroom door. See you assholes, I thought. But, I was sad. I had this warped way of not wanting to make anyone unhappy. And, my dad would be unhappy. My mom would be unhappy. They were complicated.

I had grandparents in Indiana. They were Mennonite, lived without TV or radio, but they had a fridge, a phone. They would let me stay there. They wouldn't ask questions. They were pacifists and wouldn't invite conflict. If they needed an answer, I'd blame myself, say I was into drugs. Adults over thirty seemed to think everyone in high school was crazed for drugs. I could make up all kinds of side-effects and withdrawal symptoms. They wouldn't know. I couldn't tell them.

After work on my last day, Muriel drove me and Julie to Dairy Isle, a peninsula in blacktop, with an orange corrugated roof and a statue of a doughy boy clutching a cone and licking his own face with a sickly pink tongue. Surrounded by picnic tables, it was bathed in yellow bug light and black flies. Muriel stayed in the car, her eyes unfocused, sipping a peanut butter-oreo-ba-nana-milkshake—her own invention. Julie was pissed because Muriel hadn't told her about the abortion. They'd been arguing since after we got off work at Captain Black's.

"I'm your fucking best friend," said Julie.

"And, it's fucking bad news. Did you really want to know about it?"

"You would tell freak-face over there."

"I just had to get it off my fucking chest. It doesn't matter who I told," said Muriel.

"I think I'm going to get out and stretch my legs," I said.

Crystal knew our hang-out and had parked nearby. I got in Crystal's car and she handed me a beer and turned down her Ozzy. The Buick's interior was deep red and her Betty Boop key chain dangled from the ignition.

She said, "Man, I love days when I don't have to work! That place is shit." She began laughing nervously. She wasn't even talking, just laughing.

I looked at the rain gutters, buckets filled at the edge of the building. Crystal's ashtray overflowed. I felt I might vomit. I rolled down the window and hung an arm into the cool air.

Everyone who was sipping their shakes, spooning up ice cream seemed identical, burdened. I began to cry and Crystal went uncharacteristically silent. I didn't care. We all seemed filled to the brim with shit, ready to split apart, walking around with unspoken weight, the silence an equalizer. I spilled it about the abortion, went on about shitty homophobes and pubic lice. I stuttered about gang rapes. I felt on fire, and raised my hand to my face trying to cool the flush. Fuck it. There was no going back. I had split apart, like the cracked asphalt in the heat of the sun.

"My Dad's a pedophile," I said.

"Gross," she said.

"My sister tried to commit suicide."

Crystal started laughing. She laughed so hard her fake-tanned face looked like the Dairy Isle roof.

Muriel came by and leaned down into the car. "What are you two talking about?" She looked at Crystal who was trying not to make eye contact. "What's going on?" she said, dropping her voice. Her face drained to the gray of tainted cream, her eyes widening at me.

"You're dead," she said. I was.

I watched the cars pass on the main drag, fading lights making their way out of town, and snaking on through fields and woods, cutting a map away from here. They were all bending around curves, leading to the new place. I kept repeating my secrets, already feeling new.

Take Him to Task!

Zachary Amendt

Bryce checked the mailbox on his way back from the swap meet, gripping a greasy brown bag of apple fritters between his teeth. A coupon had arrived in the mail, along with the past-due bills and the magazine subscriptions he bought with Lani's airline miles – 2,144, not enough to redeem even for a prop-engine flight from McMinnville to Bozeman – one day before they expired.

Task Casino!
100% Bingo Credit Match
(Speed Bingo only; maximum $40 deposit)

"Sweetheart, look," Bryce said, showing her. "Free money."

He used to bring her back flowers from the swap meet. Now, he only brought home donuts. Still, it was amazing what a fritter did for her morale. It was almost New Year's; the house payment was due; they were short $850. Lani was sad Christmas, not her favorite holiday but the most festive one, was over. Their tree, which had died faster than in previous years – brittle and dry with weeks still left on her Advent Calendar – was nevertheless up and decorated, lights blazing. Bryce had bought the $30 cheaper Douglas instead of a Noble Fir, and when he asked for a fresh cut he was rebuffed. The tree leaned; they named it Pisa. The mistletoe, however, was green.

"Get me the scissors, will you," he said.

Underneath the fine coupon print was even finer print: *Odds of winning: 35:1*. It was more complicated than telling Lady Luck that they needed a little help. Bryce was a gambler but more on sports — totals and spreads and money-lines — and less on slots and table games. At first his gambling was a $5 a day habit, like smoking. He liked sports because they were uncomplicated, whereas card games like Pai Gow were too nuanced and slow for him.

"You can't win," Lani said. "Not with those odds."

"Someone has to."

"You never do," she added.

"I'm supporting a local business."

"What about the local business that is our household?"

"Look, if we do win like..." Bryce examined the pixelated picture of the woman on the front of the coupon... "Miss Catherine K. of Bellevue, that's the mortgage, right there."

That monthly burden again. They were upside-down on the house already, the price of re-financing before interest rates sank to zero. Once they realized all that went into homeownership, it made them wish they were still renting.

"Or you can ask your family to help," he added.

Lani's family were not helpful. They gave support, yes, and valuable trinkets and heirlooms — such as the Rembrandt etching, stored in bubble wrap underneath their bed, too valuable to hang on the wall — but never money.

Bryce's voice went up an octave. "You think the money will just poof, materialize?" He went around the house fishing in the usual places — between the couch cushions zipped up in clear plastic she had installed to protect the sofa, her purse — scrabbling for loose change or crumpled up bills. His interior aesthetic was a strange taxidermy: antlers festooned with baseball caps, deer he didn't kill.

"What do you know about Speed Bingo?" she said.

"As much as $40 will teach me."

"You know how I react to cigarette smoke."

"Look at this picture," he said. "No one is smoking in the coupon."

They continued debating about it as she went upstairs to pee. She was conditioned to leave the seat up for him afterwards, as a courtesy. If you *were* to gamble, she felt, you should lay the game that will solve all of your debt if you win. Like lotto. But she knew it would feel strange to win that large a sum, like getting a hole-in-one on a mulligan. It wouldn't count.

"I don't want to go," she said.

"How else are we going to win it?"

"The old fashioned way: work. Sell more swimming pools."

"I can't force them to buy."

"You can't seem to convince them, either."

Pools, it turns out, did not sell themselves in Oregon, where there were two seasons: wet and dry.

"We wouldn't have to gamble on our future if you didn't mind raffling off your past."

The Rembrandt.

"Not this crap again," Lani said. "You know it's priceless."

"Then why'd you get it appraised?"

"For insurance purposes!"

Life was stressful in a one-income household. Lani looked outside, studying the daylight astutely. The facts hit her harshly: her front yard looked like it was shrinking. Her garden had failed. She seemed to have a brown thumb, despite all of the rain. The yardwork made her hands rough, as if she had spilled super glue on them. It was a lack of purpose, along with joblessness and the despair of being voluntarily under house arrest, *not to mention* her inability to find the success her sister found, as the author of important anti-cockfighting legislation back in Ohio. And all Lani knew about gambling was that the sharps waited to the last minute to gobble up the lines. What's winning, or a million?

Unless you have five times that there was no point in being rich. Did Bryce actually think it would fall in his favor like one of those Community Chest bank errors during a game of Monopoly? And losing, wasn't losing like the nausea of a vitamin on an empty stomach? All money was fake money, play money. When Bryce lost big his only regret was that he didn't have more of it to blow. Once they had won $5,000 on the Cricket World Cup, and before Lani could say *'put it in a high-yield CD,'* Bryce had blown it all on tinting the windows on their Subaru.

He pulled the car around and defrosted the windows. Two trash cans partially blocked their driveway. Winning isn't exactly providing for your family, but Lani couldn't shoehorn him into providence, so it was easier to relent, go along and avoid a fight. Perhaps it would be fun, and they might get lucky. Maybe there was a no-smoking section. As she had sat on the edge of the bed and watched him dress that morning, in cargo pants with lots of pockets for all those swap meet treasures – he was handsome, it seemed, only when it was necessary – she remembered when she was confident that she had eradicated all vestiges of the bachelor in him. Being married for as long as they had been – ten years, come March – was like being on a diet of saltpeter, and the rare times they did make love it was a question not of resisting urges but masking them as necessities. Still, it wasn't all terrible; Bryce seemed to have found the winning formula. He kept secrets from her. That's how their marriage succeeded. Secrets were the secret.

"It's against the ordinance to put the trash bins out this early," Bryce fumed. "Have you noticed how the neighbors are encroaching on our parking spot? I may leave them a firmly worded note."

They got on the I-5 freeway, which narrowed to two lanes outside of Salem. Lani herself was a good driver, a better navigator, and a terrific parallel parker. Her job, as passenger, was to

DJ, while Bryce focused on the road, fiddling with his side and rearview mirrors.

"Ah, Neil Diamond," she said. Cracklin' Rosie. Her favorite. "I wonder if he ever gets tired of singing it," she ventured.

Bryce was cut-off by a big rig. He cursed and hit the steering wheel with his palm, feebly triggering the horn.

"You don't get tired of singing it in the shower for free, so why would he get tired?"

It was one of those days where they caught all of the red lights. Not an unlucky day, just not the smoothest ride. But for these small jaunts in the car she rarely saw Bryce in profile. He had gone gray in the temples before she did, but he had more hair, and was a little fitter, whereas joblessness was making her midsection gelatinous. He was working 60 hours a week – the new normal, these days – but in sales (especially in commission jobs) nothing was guaranteed. Bryce amused his bosses with his nauseating optimism and obstinacy, his density, his dumb questions. While he was out traveling and visiting accounts Lani tried to stay busy, run errands, be among people: at the 99 cent store she saw beautiful people, people tired, people hungover, people digging sleep out of their eyes, people working, poor people, entitled people, people traveling for work, loners, *people* people, most of them in sunglasses, as if they were each, all of them, in need of a great deal of personal obscurity.

They exited the freeway in a residential district. Seemingly every other house in McMinnville was for sale or rent. The mayor had recently planted trees in the medians so the neighborhood kids couldn't play football or Frisbee between the one-way streets.

"Living here is like deciding which WalMart you want to live closest to," he observed.

McMinnville was, Lani acknowledged, a hard town to live in and even harder to sell a swimming pool in, let alone build one, all alone.

"Oh! That house is adorable," Lani said, pointing at a Craftsman.

"I wonder if they know about the kennel going in next door," he said.

"Why didn't we get a fixer-upper?"

"I guess at some point you're just... patching up the patches."

The tragedy was that there was no tragedy in Lani's life. Some hardship would have added dimension to her. Instead she got a soft landing, like a down comforter, or easy street. She had met Bryce at a large university in Ohio with a robust sports program. She wanted out of school as fast as possible; he was taking a fifth year in ROTC and he looked good in uniform, while the other boys were in wrinkled shirts and sandals and unbathed. It was possible that, if anything, Bryce communicated too well with women. He didn't want to be on any of the athletic teams but rather inside the college mascot outfit, a Thunderbird, doing backflips and mad antics in front of the TV cameras. Lani compared this to the man he was today: going the speed limit in the fast lane, careful in all of the wrong spots. When he discussed business opportunities with her, why did it sound like the latest Ponzi scheme? Work and sport is how he measured his life, while she measured hers by yards of cloth as she crocheted baby blankets for friends, none for herself.

"Remember when..."

"Yes?"

She was trying to remember herself.

"... when our biggest troubles were that our register at the Student Union Co-Op was short $20?"

"Those were the days," he said.

"I think I would trade all of the skills on my resume for just a little clairvoyance."

Glass ceilings were not made of brittle windows. She didn't need an advanced lesson in failure, but it kept coming. She felt like she was setting new records for inconsequentiality every day.

The want ads didn't always used to look like obituaries, applying and applying until she was no longer inured to rejection as she once had been. It used to be so easy to find work. Land of plenty. Of course everything in college came easy: she still had her looks. It was her figure that got Bryce's attention – at first, at least – though that's not what kept him calling her and hanging around. They had first met at a big fraternity party. They were a rambunctious couple that night, roughhousing in the greenhouse just off campus where some esoteric research on butterflies was being conducted. And for the second time in a large lecture hall. Econ 215. There were many seats but she chose the one next to him; she had to; the only left-handed desks were at the ends of the aisles.

The Task reservation – which melded seamlessly with unincorporated McMinnville – had its own police and fire departments. Weaving through the vast expanse of property were man-made estuaries where the tribal elders dumped old greyhounds they had retired from the racetrack built in 1989, with their sovereignty.

The breeze outside was preening. Mother Nature seemed to do all of her parenting in the winter. Bryce didn't like the outskirts of McMinville much, even though it had pretty post offices and quaint orthodox churches. They passed four bail bondsmen (she counted) and a string of motels, now defunct.

"Did you see that?" he said.

"What?"

"How'd you miss it? It was one of those space-agey Jetsons signs. From the 60s."

"The 1960s?"

"What other sixties would I be talking about?"

It was not Lani's decade; besides, thinking of it only made her more jealous of the America she could never know, when it seemed like they traded stocks just to have enough ticker tape on hand for the heroes' homecomings. Truly, playing the stock market was no better; those poor men at the racetrack almost had a better chance of 'hitting it big'. Maybe Bryce was right: that it was more fun to live outside of the budget, that the next wager will be kinder, that gambler's fortunes can change overnight. Momentum was just too ephemeral to measure.

Task was a cotillion of grown men. It was also the only casino Lani had ever seen with windows. At endless rows of slots eager aspirants fed the machines money as if they were squeezing a tube of toothpaste. The ashtrays were filled with what seemed like fragrant cat litter, and wads of gum stuck on the walls, in the carpet.

She and Bryce followed the arrows to BINGO and sat down at a large rectangular bar built around a cage with numbered ping pong balls sucked out through a vacuum and a staff of four proctors, making change and collecting bingo cards. The only empty seats were next to a gentleman attached to an oxygen tank who, when a waitress approached with a Gin and Tonic, emptied out the bowl of popcorn in front of him, poured in his G&T, and iced his right hand in it.

On one of the seven TVs mounted around the bingo center, a college football bowl game was in the fourth quarter, and close. Cheerleaders for both teams were lined up on the sidelines in parkas. Lani watched football in the hopes for a gaffe, or a fake play, or a wardrobe malfunction. She didn't understand why players couldn't control their emotions, why they had to spike the ball in front of or on the torso of their opponents instead of calmly handing it to the referee or else punting it into the stands as a souvenir. Then again, she had never scored a touchdown, or anything close to it, her entire life.

"If they want them to dress more risqué then they should play in warmer climates," G&T man said.

"I had fingernails before this game started," Bryce said.

"It would be nice to watch a football game that he doesn't have a bet on," Lani ventured.

This life was not so sublime to her, these days of cheap, fleeting thrills. These were people for whom winning was not a need, but a want, a must.

Inside the BINGO cage, a proctor called out the selections, holding his microphone like it was a rattlesnake.

"B14."

"Me! Me!' a woman shouted.

The announced pool was $300.

"Might as well be 33 cents," Lani accidentally said aloud.

She was learning the gambler's etiquette. People were as interesting losing money as they were on full moons. The good customers bussed their ashtrays, and the veterans wanted to be treated with 10% discounts and deference, as if they all had won Silver Stars – won, not earned. Still, the Native American tribe operating Task – the Augustines – would hang their tribal flag above the Stars and Stripes if there weren't so many military present. It surprised Lani how helpful the staff were, magnanimous and warm, the waitresses roving around the floor with lipstick on their teeth. She was mesmerized, overstimulated. Too many numbers and lights running across her eyes. The casino looked a bit off to her, like a silent film that had been hastily colorized. Plus, her bingo cards were ice cold. The prospect of winning was like that one machine in the university arcade with the hundreds of quarters perched precariously at the edge of the precipice with the metal broom seemingly pushing them imperceptibly toward the edge… that it was just a matter of one well-placed quarter or a surreptitious tilt of the machine and it's all yours, jackpot, and yet it was never yours, or Lani's.

"Bryce, look down real quick," she said, tugging at his shirt.

Better than a jackpot, it was an ignition key to a BMW.

"Leave it," he said.

"No," she said. "At our feet are the keys to someone's car. I don't know what car. I would have to scour the parking lot to find the car." She bent down to pick it up. "But I have the key now."

"Let's find the Lost and Found," he said.

"It's my car," Lani said. "I can go anywhere."

They stayed at Task for five hours, winning, losing, breaking even. A phantom offsides in the Western Kentucky game cost Bryce $3,000, and Lani lacked the heart to say she was sorry – she would have just picked another incorrect outcome, and besides, he had been so patient with her the entire marriage, had never reproached her, not after her parking ticket scam cost her the cushy babysitting job in Salem, not even as they garnished his wages to pay her thefts back, not even after she was laid off at Applebee's because she claimed she was robbed taking the evening till to the bank, and not after she was fired at the dentist's office for (inadvertently) exchanging counterfeit money. She felt she had finally connected the dots that were the archipelago of the events that got them here, in this very casino, where upon exiting, the automatic doors violently opening, Lani unwittingly disposed her gum into a winning lottery scratcher. Plain bad luck, but you can't be upset, the stadium empties, everyone goes home. Except Task, open all night, every day.

The drive home felt like those somber flights to Portland from Las Vegas in years past. Either they had lost it all and were sad, or had won big but were too tired to celebrate.

"It could be worse," Bryce said. "We could have gambled away our vacation homes like that Hollywood writer."

"Which one?"

"The guy with all the vacation homes in Florida."

"Vacation houses aren't homes. What about our mortgage?" Bryce smiled.

"I guess that's what payday loans are for."

He dropped Lani off at the house and made a last run to the liquor store before it closed. She needed time, time alone, to herself, as if given a few hours she could figure out her whole life. Like she could get her life together in that or any span of time. She was not married to Bryce: she was married to a game of chance. Theirs were not shallow problems but deep end problems. The winner no longer takes all these days, and the losers get a larger share every year. She was jealous that Bryce's life was so simple and alliterative – football and feelings – and upset that the coffee tasted better, the cigarettes sharper, after he won, until he gradually lost back his winnings. Not losing, that is: *hemorrhaging* money.

He came home with too nice of a bottle of tequila, just in time for the broadcast from Times Square. With Ryan Seacrest and Dick Clark, there was no reason why there couldn't be a little romance, a kiss at midnight. Bryce fished about for a candle to set the mood, but all he found were birthday candles leftover from her Over-the-Hill party.

"I have a big question for you," she said at 11:57 p.m.

"Big, or heavy?"

"Heavy."

"Oh Lani. I want to end the year on a high note."

"Just give me this."

"Ok."

"What's your biggest beef?"

"Beef?"

"Beef. Grievance. With me."

"If I had to pick one," he said, "I think it's that I became the husband you wanted, not the husband I wanted to be."

A wife, she knew, was a sparring partner, a partner in crime, a cribbage nemesis. But she was something else altogether.

"If only one of us was miserable," she said, five seconds before 2009 A.D., "then we could make it work."

Bryce lifted his drink. Three seconds.

"To a marriage on the rocks," he said, as the ball dropped.

"No," she said. "On ice."

It was good tequila. *Repasado* means 'old' in Spanish. *Anejo* means rested. Greyhounds can't swim.

Recitations

Marko Vignjevic

The Drive

A derelict parker picked up his car at the impound lot. Having paid the sum designated by the Traffic Court, he claimed his vehicle. After voicing his suspicions as to the damage to the paint job he was assured he'd better drive away. Cursing into the rear view mirror the derelict parker merged with the traffic which was in all tolerable. He halted at a red light and was approached by a volunteer car attendant with a rag and squeegee in his hands. The motorist gestured that the wretch move along aided by the traffic light turning yellow. Ahead, on his destined route, there was a street car plowing along its rails. The derelict driver yielded to the electric conveyance doing so in neutral. Once the street car had passed, lo and behold a prospect of a lane change opened up. He cut off the car moving in parallel to his and positioned himself on a diagonal. Not faltered of determination he drove on. He was all smiles at the wheel which for reasons unknown to him fell off in his hands. Not knowing what to do or how to go about doing it, the derelict parker kept on going. So nervous was he that he began biting the steering wheel in the hope that the road would straighten out; he was also thinking of the practicality of the afore-mentioned street car. His fellow motorists began honking their horns at him having noticed the driving implausibility of his situation which

made the derelict parker feel self-conscious. Rushed to think
and still commanding the steering wheel as if it mattered, he
came to a notion of straddling the curb which was not far in
front of him. It was only then that he stopped his car, got out
with the steering wheel gnawed up in his hands. Much to his
relief no one noticed his predicament until the air bag deployed.

Teeth

Candied apples and cotton candy were all for naught as regarded
Mr. Sila. A man of an otherwise adventurous appetite, Mr. Sila was
deficient in one aspect of oral apparel – his teeth. Seeing how he
couldn't afford artificial teeth due to a chronic failure at job hunt-
ing the cause of which were his toothless gums, Mr. Sila would
find sustenance in liquefied foods. Set in his ways of both diet
and lifestyle in general, while going through the newspaper one
morning Mr. Sila read an ad for a restaurant space to rent. He set
about the task of becoming self-employed and hence composed
a business plan which he intended to present to the bank for the
purposes of acquiring a loan. The business plan consisted of found-
ing an establishment which would only serve blended or liquefied
food, beverages not excluded. "Don't smile at the bank.".-, Mr. Sila
kept repeating to himself as he was walking into a local branch of
the bank. The bank approved his loan and the papers were signed.
Mr. Sila made an appointment with the proprietor, commencing
with the initial transaction and the formalities of the transfer of
the first payment installment. Not three weeks later Mr. Sila's
restaurant had its grand opening; he called the place Zub. It became a fad in the city immediately, it then grew into a trend and
further developed into a blown out craze. Finally Mr. Sila could
afford artificial teeth but he dared not risk it for fear he would be
perceived as a culinary counter-revolutionary by his patrons.

Backstep

Mara is turning thirty years old. Nothing seems to be helping her state of mind, brought to the brink even more so by a sneaking suspicion that time will only speed up from this point on. She's looking into a laughing mirror in the bathroom, managing to find a childish grin in the corner of her mouth. After dutifully dispensing with attiring for the morning in a dress of her choice, girlish as it is, Mara walks out. She has people to see and places at which to be seen. Unlike the ease of this sunny day there is an ache in her ankles as yet laboring about the business of ensuring she meets her friends on time for a birthday breakfast. Shouts are heard upon their meeting and they take their seats at a table. Not realizing why, Mara feels uneasy having once noticed that the birthday cake the waiter served had no birthday candles on it; even the presents she's opening appear to be thirty years old. For a while Mara braved through, an undertaking aided by champagne which she is enjoying only until she notices how wrinkled the tin foil wrapping around the bottle neck is. But as someone said, "Life begins at thirty," and with that in mind and by means of her own interpretation, Mara raises her glass in a toast, speaking: *I'm as young today as I'll ever be.*

Making Mondays

Upon recalling an experience which never came to full fruition, Gero Gerai made ready his circumstances to be. He did so by implementing a practice soon to become a habit. The practice was simple: nothing was to be repeated except Mondays. He began by doing outlandish things: speaking unruly words in odd sentences; dressing in extravagant ways; approaching anyone who caught his eye and conversing with them. He did all those things every day except Monday. And though his new behavioral pattern played havoc with his standing at work, Gero Gerai's dispositions (which varied from day to day) were accepted by his coworkers. In the months that followed he acquainted himself with various cohorts and strata of society. Gero became a regular fixture in many lives from those of matrons, postmen and ushers to those of artists, politicians and ambassadors. Every day became a carnival and he was the fore-bearer of it, every day except Monday. And if one could look into the future one would surely see Gero Gerai in his finest clothes, on his favorite street, going to his favorite restaurant to meet with no one new, entirely inconspicuous, in all unnoticeable as if he left the world locked in his apartment and one would know its Monday.

The Puppeteer

On a designated corner of the street, amid the pedestrian traffic, a puppet danced at the command of its handler's expression. There was a shoe box by his side intended for those among the passersby who happened to be in high spirits. The puppeteer didn't speak or sing, the only audible thing was the sound of the puppet's wooden feet resonating on the pavement into a meager distance. He returned to the same spot every day regardless of the weather and pulled on the strings of his obedient employee. The puppeteer would take brakes of a toilet nature in the court yard of a nearby building the front door of which was always left open. Being a street performer he also carried business cards with him which he would hand out to interested parties who were planning their children's birthday. That's how the puppeteer made his living until a sunny winter's day when a doll collector saw him on the same corner conducting his puppet on the slush of yesterday's snowfall. The man engaged the puppeteer in solicitation for his wooden prop. And while the street performer's stance on the matter was at first firmly negative a sudden gust of the winter wind made him relent and the transaction was made. Ever since that street corner stands vacant while the puppeteer roams through the city looking to buy a new puppet with the money he made in a sale he cannot forget which kept depleting in sum and value it once had in his mind.

Echo

Whatever Barbarez would say someone was there to repeat it. It appeared he was a man of some significance to everyone but himself. Barbarez knew there must be a way to make good use of this phenomenon. Through making certain well placed enquiries it came to his attention that all who knew him or knew of him thought he looked like a lot of people and that's why all the attention. Apparently Barbarez looked not only like historical figures but also like your next door neighbor and other individuals who belonged to the species of acquaintance. Having ascertained this to be a fact, all be it a one he made peace with unwillingly, Barbarez began choosing his words and topics of conversation very carefully, for his previous attempt to profit from his hapless talent by charging people for advice failed and it failed because everyone knew that advice would come to them whether they paid for it or not. So came to be a period in the city hence referred to as The Silence of Barbarez. That's what brought about his estrangement from his wife and friends. During that period he kept to himself, reluctant to answer the most benign questions. Barbarez grew weary of people thus becoming a regular absentee from all the social events which drew even more attention to his condition. But there was one person who eventually broke his silence and overall asocial behavior – it was his wife. Something of Barbarez must've rubbed off on her over the years, and having once gotten through his hardened aura she made him see that if you look like a lot of people there's more room for you for no one can in fact see who you truly are.

The Stain

At a table in a restaurant, dining with her gentleman friend, Dorotea stained her silk blouse. She realized it much later during desert and was perfectly angry with him for not noticing it and mentioning it to her. Dorotea found this absence of attention on his part to be a sign of a conceited man and someone who will never appreciate her, how could he when he didn't even see the damage done to her blouse which she chose to wear especially for him. Sitting through the remainder of the last course, Dorotea was politely looking at him. Suddenly, no matter what he would say she would hear a lie and in his outward appearance she began seeing flaws. Dorotea was amazed that he didn't even perceive her state of mind, and when they settled their bill, in walking out the restaurant door, Dorotea, inspired by seeing him outside among other people, began reprimanding herself and a while later hating him for making her feel that way. However despondent, Dorotea allowed him to walk her to her door all the while not saying a word which he thought was a symptom of her fascination with him, and why should've she said anything when in her eyes he had become that stain which ruined her blouse, and one doesn't talk to stains. Once in front of her building, as he was about to kiss her, Dorotea gave voice pulling back:
-Never before, never after.

The Roundabout

Headed for a full dead stop, a line of cars came onto the roundabout. The habitual circle which served solely as a conduit to someplace else was in urgent need of repair and it being the day those repairs were to begin, the city authorities announced it was to be closed off. From another junction there arrived marathon runners also entering the roundabout. Both they and that line of cars were made to move in circles, for their exit routs of choice and plan had been closed off. There was only a single one way street left open leading to the roundabout through which a long string of bicyclists entered the roundabout therefore partaking in the futile exercise of the orbiting marathon runners and that line of cars. Starting off as strangers, they soon became acquaintances when after a while they found out that there was no way out. After the authorities closed off the last street, behind the roadblocks of every prong leading into the roundabout the crews of workmen meant to commence with the repairs were standing in wait along with other citizenry. Eventually those cars in the line ran out of gas; the runners were taken away by ambulances, and the organizers of the bicycle race proclaimed a winner so as to appease their competitive nature. And even while the repairs were carried out, the roundabout remained a circle irrespective of the fact no one was circling around it.

The Obituary

Mr. Plam was finishing with his morning newspaper when he came across an obituary of another Mr. Plam. He read it and learned the time and place of the man's funeral. His interest in the other Mr. Plam was heightened by the coincidence that the deceased man looked exactly like the still living Mr. Plam which is why that observer of a stranger's death decided to attend Mr. Plam's funeral. He arrived to an oddly busy cemetery, trying to ascertain which of the many funeral processions was in the honor of his Mr. Plam. The still living Mr. Plam positioned himself in front of the chapel at the end of a line of mourners. A woman who moved up next to him as the line was entering the chapel asked Mr. Plam did he know Mr. Plam to which he answered no and stepped back and away from the line and the altogether eerie conditions. Mr. Plam did however walk with the mourners to lay Mr. Plam to his eternal resting place. He followed the gravediggers once they concluded the burial and enquired as to the date when the head stone will be put up. Mr. Plam left the cemetery when they gave him the date. Days passed and while they did so he thought about Mr. Plam's chance demise, but no one can die in Caesar's stead. He postponed going to Mr. Plam's grave to see the head stone. On the other hand he wanted to read what they wrote on Mr. Plam's last ornament. It was a plain Tuesday when he found himself standing over Mr. Plam's grave whose head stone read: PLAM – BARELY.

Livid Leon

Unnerved to the point of bursting a capillary a day, Leon lived known to everyone as a spiteful man. Criticizing everything, it was as if the mere notion of the world bothered him. There were days when Leon would take a break and abstain from his colorful commentary. But still, no matter how few and far between those days were, the people who knew him best avoided him the most. That being thus, Leon would seek a new platform for his coward's rage and it was always topical with him. The bulk of those topics on which no one dwelled longer than the weather report Leon found in the news. He was so irritable that everything became a disinhibitor to him making his tongue, much like his character, more acid. A product of nothing except his own hurt pride and a vanity completely denied, Leon lived the prophecy which would never be fulfilled that a time will come when only one man will be right and the rest consigned to abject erroneousness of their lives. And while Leon continued set in his ways, ever hating the lack of understanding on the part of those he would judge and judge harshly, the world was tightening around him in a manner binding. Forever to remain in an endless fume and fright, livid Leon disappeared one day and the people who once knew him got word that he was last seen on a barren mountain top cheering on a passing comet and they knew he was happy.

Diving High

Waking up at an agreeable hour and with the sun beaming through her shutters in tasseled rays of the first daylight, Magda stretched her toes as a sure sign that she shan't move, but rather lounge about in bed. In a motion which seemed to last for a hundred years she turned on her back 'till further enveloped in the covers of the fatigue past. Magda perceived a sinking sensation and orchestrated her breathing pattern accordingly, affording herself plentiful effects. She dove further and higher still, infusing her senses with an invisible liquid distilled during the hours of slumber she had found the night before. There was no emission of plans from within her mind, at least not for today. Magda neither projected nor disseminated speculations of a kind she dreamt she could do without such as work and any prefabricated obligations. Magda took no notice of the movement of sunbeams on her wall; it was only the dive she abided. Dismissing the possibility of resisting the lounging about her gentle sheets and tender pillow, Magda felt her bed was ingesting her. Gone were the street noises and those of electrical charges otherwise explicit to all morning routines Magda had surrendered to a future day, for the pillow wrapped its indentation's edges around her ears. She rose on a high where the early air was tactile and the space around her bed presented her with a window beyond which the world was diving with her.

Musing On a Jockey

He was always the one riding in a red polka dot shirt. At the best of times he would come in second, he never got the chance to punch the air with a clenched fist; all he would ever do after crossing the finish line was pat the side of his horse's neck. Iris lost count of how much money she squandered betting on her jockey in the red polka dot shirt, all Iris knew is that she was madly in love with him. Whenever he would squat in a stride her heart would drop and Iris would, 'till further future comes, be lost to the world. Men of enviable standing in society would approach her in the stands of the hippodrome and Iris would deny them all. The winters she found particularly hard due to the race track being closed. Many a time she tried to find him outside of that venue, but to her dismay no one knew anything about him. If horseracing was the sport of kings then she would be queen even if it would take the rest of her life. As was her custom when the last snow thawed that year, Iris was in the stands looking through her binoculars – she didn't see him. Iris checked the race forms once more scrolling down the list of names with her index finger hoping to find out why he wasn't in the gates when the paper on her lap began to darken from a shadow. It was her jockey who was standing next to her. Iris knew it was him because she was wearing a red polka dot dress that day.

The Best Possible Nothing

One minute into the outside and Trovar noticed that absolutely everything looked the same. Every span of street and vehicle; every building; every local; every establishment and every person walking in or out of it were replicated to infinity which only he perceived. But just to make sure, Trovar investigated further by walking into stores of whatever type where he found that each article, regardless of its purpose, was indeed but another unit of something someone made though he didn't know when and why. A further probing into his surroundings revealed to Trovar that the people as well were not only of a same dress but moreover of a same mind and body. The day proceeded to unwind in a familiar pattern whereby upon Trovar's arrival at the office he found that all his coworkers had the same job. It was with great difficulty that Trovar accepted this new reality and yet somehow he didn't stand out. When he would voice an opinion he would realize his friends thought the exact same thing; whatever his body language, Trovar noticed the same body language in other people. That night he met his girlfriend at a restaurant where he realized that all the patrons were dining on the same dish and what was worse she looked like every woman there. The world had exhausted all variety and distinction of life; -it ended and no one knew it.

Angry At Strawberries

Gina grew strawberries in her back yard. Those she couldn't eat she would take to market to sell which was an additional means of supporting herself and meager though it was because of those strawberries Gina was approached by a man who had a business proposition for her. The venture put forth by that gentleman involved Gina making as many strawberry derivatives and related products for which he said there was a burgeoning market due to an increased demand for organic, homegrown produce. Gina accepted his offer and in addition to family recipes she came up with a few of her own for the company she began running. Eventually a problem developed with Gina: -aside from the wealth her business brought her, for reasons of the ubiquitousness of strawberries in her life she stopped eating them, a dietary void supplemented over time with Gina's loathing of strawberries. She gave interviews and appeared at trade shows in the capacity of speaker, but when she did have time Gina would order her chauffeur to drive her to the house which she had sold once her business took off and there she would stand in front of the rear gate looking at what was once her strawberry plot now covered in weeds. Doing so a thought permeated her mind and Gina spoke in a whisper —*what doesn't feed me doesn't need me.*

Lost Kamelia

A shoemaker by vocation, Kamelia set out to make herself a pair of shoes in which she would never get lost. They needed to be comfortable yet with an aesthetic which was in line with the most formal of occasions, they also had to be durable; to fit every street so to speak. Kamelia dug so deep inside of herself seeking inspiration that she forgot about the world around her. Becoming ever more fixated on the idea of the perfect shoe, she never went out of her workshop, so Kamelia had all of her life's necessities delivered to her. She would labor late into the night many of which she spent sleepless and even when the occasional dream would fall in her charge the dream was always about shoes and she would immediately wake up and start drawing the design she saw during her slumber. Renderings of her visions were piling up throughout her workshop in all manner of paper and over time she came up with the ultimate solution for her shoe. It didn't take her long to craft the shoes and when they were finished Kamelia found they were a perfect fit and just the right kind of appeal; she was sure she would never get lost in them. Having decided to take her new shoes out for a walk and once in the street, she caught a glimpse of herself in a store window. She couldn't believe what a wreck she had become and then and there Kamelia knew she was lost.

Minding Minutes

The morning of his departure came and Petronius called for a cab to take him to the airport. It being the middle of winter, Petronius made mental provisions for getting to his gate a bit late. He was waiting in front of his building, suitcase in hand, when the cab pulled up and throughout the drive Petronius was constantly looking at his watch. When he arrived to the airport he learned that all the flights have been delayed and over the course of the wait Petronius found himself amidst the other passengers who in time and unlike him settled along the floor. Keeping up the habit which had its purpose in the cab, that is constantly checking the time, Petronius made the mistake of minding minutes while waiting. He did nothing except look at his watch the clock face of which had lost all expression and the hands didn't manage to advance along its circumference. It became a battle of time and tolerance in which Petronius found allies in those in the wait who asked him how long has it been. In due time everyone fell asleep except Petronius still on his noncommissioned post in the capacity of the keeper of no one's time. As they boarded the plane, once seated Petronius looked at his watch once more before takeoff and peering into those notches designating the minutes he wandered how could something so small last forever.

Corner Guard

On a Friday yet to pass, the tenants of a building which stood on the street corner gathered for an emergency meeting. Among other things, the minutes of that meeting included their unanimously expressed wish to prevent people from meeting and loitering on their street corner. They drafted a letter doing so hastily which they submitted to the municipal authorities. After further consideration the powers at be decided in the tenants' favor under the condition that they must keep watch over that street corner. The new custom having been installed, the tenants took turns standing guard on their street corner, approaching whatever outsider who found themselves there waiting for someone. The more avid among them even reported those strangers to the police and word began circulating through the city of the infamous street corner. In time the tenants' new custom became a prohibition to others who avoided that street corner. Pleased that their initiative yielded results, the tenants thought their work was done, -so they stopped guarding their street corner. But they had forgotten the terms which conditioned their new custom. Even now they take turns on that street corner only there's no one there to guard the corner against but having been granted a right they have also taken on an obligation the fruitlessness of which mattered to no one but them.

Yawning

For reasons unknown to him, Varan spent most of his days yawning. When this new trait of his first came into being, Varan wanted to know the cause of it and as is the case with all personality traits once enough time goes by one accepts them as sure as Varan accepted his yawning. There was a drawback to his unwanted habit, namely because of it he never did well at job interviews which would always start out fine until the yawning began. And those other infrequent jobs he did have Varan was fired from because of his yawning which made him come off as not quite the go-getter. But while sitting in a café one well-lit day drinking his coffee one of Varan's yawns drew the attention of a modeling scout. The woman approached him and said he had beautiful teeth and later, after she sat down with him the scout told Varan he could do amazing things in toothpaste commercials. He signed with the agency the same day and he now populates every species of media making a decent living where once there were just yawns.

The Equivalent Of Luck

The only true states of happiness are when we are children and when we are in love – the rest is just shock. An example of this was Ishtvan Ksabo who played the lottery every week, and after failing to win he would put on his best suit and tie, walk to the dumpster in the street and discard the ticket with indignation. On the night of one such televised lottery draw, Ishtvan Ksabo had to go to the bathroom and upon his return to the television set he learned he had lost again. He got dressed, tied his four-in-hand knot, took the lottery ticket and went outside to throw it in the dumpster. When he got back the same television program was on with a slight addition, the announcer of the winning ticket was making a correction and as she was doing it Ishtvan Ksabo realized it was his ticket that won. And when he heard the garbage truck emptying the dumpster outside he ran to meet and stop it, but once in the street he found that the truck was on its way along with his lottery ticket thus sending Ishtvan Ksabo into a chase down the street, screaming repetitively *-Gimme gonna get it!-*

Quitting The Weekend

Everyone at work appeared to be a bit touched in the head that day, walking through the office like fruit flies with no biological imperative. Vera was faced with the questions pertaining to the date, the time which was as if never to pass and too frequent comments on the air temperature. Vera accepted the fact that today the job of all her coworkers will be to come to terms with a new work week. Patient as she was by nature, she was under the impression they were all creeping up the gallows, and for her own part Vera felt nothing significant about that day which was precisely why everybody wanted to talk and hang around her. And she did indulge them which, truth be told, did cost her some time and nerves, playing the part of the ever designated den mother. So when quitting time came Vera was nowhere to be found, they asked among themselves but no one knew where she'd gone and until the next time round they were wasting the time that time itself wouldn't spare counting on the fact that Vera will always be there and available.

Oblivious To Mosquitoes

Where the neck meets the shoulder Maurice Maurice found a red, itchy spot one morning. He thought nothing of it and went about his day as usual. Being a sound sleeper Maurice Maurice never heard the bloodsuckers and sure enough the next morning he woke up to yet another inflamed patch of skin. A week of these assaults had to pass before Maurice Maurice began pondering the cause of his new look and even then he didn't understand it. What was worse, Maurice Maurice was so deep in denial that he sought out no remedy for those insect bites, but unlike him the mosquitoes very much believed in Maurice Maurice, feasting on him every night. It had gotten so bad that he had to see a dermatologist who confirmed those spots were in fact insect-related. But Maurice Maurice didn't accept such a diagnosis, he couldn't fathom the notion of something so small doing him harm. Maurice Maurice went to a fortune teller to find out more about those spots and was given the interpretation that his skin condition was a sign of greatness. Well pleased with such an explanation he went home in his new found glory never to make the connection between cause and effect where he remained a true God but only to mosquitoes.

Boatman's Harvest

Severed water was parting in waves at the foot of the bow as he was taking people to the opposite bank of the river. No one would talk to him so the boatman grew silent over each span of the waterway all of which began looking alike to him. The only variables were the waves and the light wind atop the surface of the river. With his back covered in a long coat he would never turn around to face his passengers sitting at the stern except to collect the toll. On any given day he would hear all breeds of language and he would see the faces of the people he would carry across in the water below while minding his pole. Those faces he did see were never to be repeated much like the voices which belonged to them, but their words did linger in the boatman's mind. And once the horizon bowed to the moon and the scarred guardian settled in its post above, he knew it was time to go home so he would tie his vessel to the dock and lay his pole to rest in the hollow of the boat. He did this every day until the time he came to the river bank and found another boatman waiting for him.

Utilities

Her company survived the crucial first few years and though taken aback by the work she had to do during that period, Tula Holtz assembled her team with the purpose of setting out a ten year plan. Of course everyone had their horse to root for: Marketing had an aggressive strategy; Financial had a restrictive budget; Sales was asking for price revision; and Operations was for investing in upgrading the company's manufacturing facilities. But Tula Holtz worried that the greater the shift the shorter the reach of her company will be;- she also knew that before you go higher you need to dig deeper for the sake of the structure's soundness. So Tula Holtz decided to invest in her own talent pool, in the payroll. The manufacturing facilities didn't need upgrading for the company was young; there will be no price revision for she didn't want her consumers revising the value of her products; the budget will be restrictive with the exception of reward by result;- and the marketing strategy will remain sustainable for fear of alienation of her core consumers. In the years that followed Tula Holtz was proven right by the company's payroll not increasing but rather by the rise of pay of every employee. Everything is a utility and so were all the departments in her company.

Prima Verita

Spring would find Irma in a very odd way wherever she might be. When the season of bloom would come, Irma would freeze in space and time, lasting the way she was until spring would pass. People would look at her stationary figure, her face caught in an otherwise fleeting expression and they would gawk at the sight of her; some would take pictures while Irma stood in the grip of spring. While in such a state of display, whether glancing at her watch, adjusting her eyeglasses or simply in mid-step, Irma didn't age for the simple fact that her person and everything about her except her heart, soul and mind would become public. But aside from all that, Irma's memory was very much alive during this condition, though she didn't feel uneasy because of it, Irma would recall certain things she saw and heard at a later time. And still when the season comes round, that messenger of spring stands as proof of change and it's different every year.

Marko Vignjevic
4/12-4/26, 2013.

Mistaken Identity

Steve Slavin

I have a rather unusual name. In fact, if you checked the residential phone listings in all five boroughs of New York, you would find just sixteen Kanadlehoppers.

You might assume that someone with a name like that must be some kind of a nerd. But nothing could be further from the truth. OK, maybe I haven't had an actual date in eleven years, but that's just because I happen to be extremely selective. Just the other day I got a call from a young woman, and I could tell from the sound of her voice that she was very attractive.

"Hello?"

"Marty?"

"This is Marty."

"Are you sure you're Marty? Marty Kanadlehopper?"

"Trust me, no one pretends to have that name."

I can hear her laughing. "I am soooo sorry. I didn't mean to laugh, but you're very funny!. Anyway, I must have the wrong number."

I didn't want her to hang up. "May I ask what you're calling about?"

"I'm afraid it's very personal. I'm sorry to have bothered you." Then she hung up.

I stared at the phone, listening to the dial tone. You know, I really should get caller ID.

Then I wondered who this other Marty Kanadlehopper could be. I had an old Brooklyn phonebook, practically a collector's item, so I looked him up. It turned out there was a Martin Kanadlehopper who lived way on the other side of Brooklyn.

A few weeks later I got a call from another woman.

"Hello?"

"Martin?"

"This is Martin."

"Martin Kanadlehopper?" Boy, this was getting old.

"The same. May I ask who's calling?"

"This is *Mrs.* Martin Kanadlehopper."

"What is this, some kind of joke?"

"I think I had better explain. No, I am certainly not married to *you!*"

"Well, I already *knew* that."

"You see, I am married to a different Martin Kanadlehopper."

"You mean, the Martin Kanadlehopper on East 93rd Street in Canarsie?"

"That is correct."

"So how can I help you?"

"Well, for some time we have been getting calls from women we don't know, plus frequent hang-ups. And since you're the only other Kanadlehopper listed in Brooklyn with a first initial, M, we would like you to consider changing your listing to *Martin* Kanadlehopper. That way, you would not be missing those calls, and my husband and I could have some peace."

"I don't think so. This was my parents' number from even before I was born. My father's name is Max."

"Look, Martin, your social life is none of my business; I am not a judgmental person. But evidently some of the women in your harem are calling our number by mistake. And just for your information, Martin and I have been happily married for eighteen years."

"Mrs. Kanadlehopper, if I told you about my social life, you wouldn't *believe* me."

"Look mister social butterfly, I'm going to level with you. I want all these phone calls to stop! I don't care how you do it. Just tell all your lady friends to stay away from my husband!" And then she slammed down the phone.

About six months later I got another call.

"Marty?"

"Yes."

"Remember me?"

It was the young woman who had been looking for the other Marty Kanadlehopper. I'd recognize that voice anywhere. That beautiful young woman.

"Of course I remember you."

"I am so flattered."

"Why, thank you."

"You're welcome!… Marty, could you do me a great big favor?"

Anything, I thought to myself. *Any*thing!

"Could you give me the other Marty's phone number. I must have misplaced it."

"As a matter of fact I can. Just give me a minute. I have an old Brooklyn phone book."

"You're an angel!"

"Thank you. By the way, may I ask you what your name is?"

"Nona."

"Nona. What a beautiful name."

"Thank you, Marty!"

"Here's the number. Area code 718, 772-0426."

"Thank you, you've been so kind."

"Wait! Nona, I need to tell you something."

"Yes?"

"I got a call from his wife."

"*Marty's* wife?"

"Yes, it was few months ago. She said that all these women were calling her husband and she demanded that the calls be stopped."

"What did *you* have to do with any calls *he* was getting?"

"How should *I* know? Besides, I'm not even related to him."

"Well, thank you for telling me. You're a sweetheart." Then she hung up.

Boy, my social life was really picking up. I might even be able to get a date out of this.

A few months later she called again. As soon as I heard her voice, I was in heaven.

"Marty?"

"Nona!"

"I am so amazed that you remembered me!"

"I will always recognize your beautiful voice."

"Well thank you! Marty, I was wondering if you could do me a big favor."

*Any*thing! *Any*thing! Just *say* the word!

"Remember how sweet you were the last time we talk-ed? Well, it turns out that Marty moved, and I don't have his new number. Is there any way you can help me figure out where he is?"

I would do anything for Nona. Even if it meant helping her find another guy.

"Look Nona, it might take me awhile, so could I call you back?"

"No, Marty. How about if I call you in an hour?"

"OK, I'll do my best."

I tried all kinds of computer searches, but no other M Kanadlehoppers turned up. I printed out a list of Kanadlehoppers all over the country, figuring that maybe he was related to some of them. When the phone rang, I was prepared.

"Marty, it's me. Could you find his new number?"

"No, I'm sorry. But I did manage to print a list of Kanadle-hoppers all over the country. Maybe he's related to one of them."

"Thank you, Marty. Look, I'm going to level with you, OK?"

"Sure."

"I know Marty's married, but I've been very discretely seeing him on the side. It's not so hard because his wife works days and he works nights for the Sanitation Department. So there are certain times when I can call him when she's not at home."

"Yeah?"

"The problem is that Marty is a complete screw-up. It's bad enough that he has other girls on the side, but *they're* the ones who are calling the house when the wife's there."

"I see."

"Anyway, I didn't hear from Marty for a while, so one morning I called him. The phone was disconnected. So I went out to where they lived. And would you believe that they moved – and left no forwarding address?"

"I'm sorry."

"Thanks, Marty. You've been so understanding."

"Nona, could I tell you something?"

"Sure."

"I would do *any*thing for you."

"Oops! Sorry, Marty, I just got another call."

I sat there staring at the receiver. I knew then that I would never get to meet this beautiful woman.

A year later I was still fantasizing about Nona. And wishing that I could have been the other Marty Kanadlehopper – except, of course, for that awful wife. As always, I got up at six a.m. and was the first one into work. As I walked down the dimly lit hallway, I saw a woman walking towards me. It was Vivian, a very sweet older woman I sometimes chatted with. She had the strangest expression on her face and she was walking very, very slowly.

"Viv, are you OK?"

"Are *you* OK?"

"Sure, I'm fine. But Viv, you look like you've just seen a ghost."

She began to shake. I led her to a chair and helped her sit down. She just kept staring at me and shaking her head.

"Should I get you some water?"

"You're *alive*, Marty! You're *alive*!"

I went into a little comic routine, patting myself all over and saying, "Yes, I'm alive! Glory be, I'm *alive*!"

"Marty, are you *really* alive?"

"Yes, Viv, I'm very *much* alive!"

"But you're supposed to be *dead*! On the way to work, I heard it on the radio. They said you were killed in some kind of traffic accident."

"Let me see if I'm hearing you correctly. They said 'Marty Kanadlehopper is dead?'"

"That's what I heard."

Just then, Jeff came down the hallway. "Marty, you've *alive*!"

"You heard it on the way to work?"

"Yeah, I know that on the news they lie all the time, but this is ridiculous!"

"Hey listen, I've got a radio in my office. Let's see if we can get some more details."

So we went into my office and I turned on WINS 1010, the all-news station. We didn't have long to wait.

"We now have an update on this story. Here is a statement from the Sanitation Commissioner about this tragic death. 'Martin Kanadlehopper worked for the Sanitation Department for twenty-one years. Last night he left his truck to assist a motorist whose car had stalled at an intersection. Witnesses saw the car lurch forward, striking him. He died before the paramedics arrived. Martin Kanadlehopper and his wife would have celebrated their twentieth wedding anniversary this Sunday. Instead, on that day, his family will bury a hero.'"

The newscaster went on to say that the driver, identified as Wynona Scott, had appeared to be in shock, and was taken under police escort to Coney Island Hospital for observation.

Letter from Hadeskap College Underground

Tantra Bensko

Sept. 30

Dear Jessica

My father always did look at me strangely when, during our little bedtime talks, I went on about my dreams of marriage to some poetic man with long hair, maybe someone who played cello, or painted scenes of wonder. Father would stand by the large painting of his black-clad brother, Dees, which as you know was right over my bed since I was thirteen years old. Father would remind me of what a great family we had, considering Father's fancy job within Canadian Security Intelligence Service, as if that put an end to my speculations of my lovely future. I didn't know why, until recently. I can't say I'm happy about it. Dees is quite handsome, with strong cheekbones and a flat stomach, but his hair is short, and he doesn't even like pretty music or bright colors in art at all. And he's pale.

But I'm keeping my chin up and my neck long, my tummy in, and my dresses clean as befits someone of my new station. I don't know why I have to wear only black now, and give up my white chiffon dress, but so be it.

Father said he had planned my marriage to Uncle Dees all along. And not just he, but the circles intersecting on the floor in his Obsidian Study charted our marriage day out too, in detail. The twenty second of September. Red and black circles with marks all the way around for the seasons, astrology, hours, all something he could spin around in his head, re-paint, and then stand in the center of, speaking in that language I didn't understand. I only saw the scene mostly when I would go in to deliver him some cake I had made in my tiny oven, or extra sweet lemonade I'd made before taking it out to sell in the stand. Once, Father was standing in the intersection of the circles. He dressed in red on one side of his body, which was positioned over the black circle, and he was wearing black on the other side, which was positioned over the red circle. He had his arms out and was making one long sound.

I think I only sold any glasses of lemonade five times, probably not my fault but just because we live so far out in the countryside. But I had a good time sitting at the stand, which I put by that grove by the road, drinking it in the hot sun, and reading fantasy books about a girl getting married and becoming a princess, though not usually a queen, like me. I always thought pretty people were princesses and ugly ones, because they're old, queens. I didn't know why my father always gave me that kind of book, but he did. I can see now he was preparing me to be the Queen Persephone of Dees' Order. Not just Queen over Vancouver's underground – because the students at the school down here are from all over BC.

Yes, I'm down here now, a married woman. A lot happened while you went off to theater camp. I'm sorry to say I won't get to see you when you get back home. I hope you had a good time, and I know how talented you are at plays. I can't wait to hear if you kissed any boys there.

I don't know why Father didn't just come out and say I was supposed to marry Uncle Dees all along. Well, I guess he knew I would have run away from home if he did. I would have gone to stay with your family – or maybe that's too obvious. Father would probably have discovered me the first day. He knows you're my best friend. And you are, love! I would have gone to live in the hollow, mossy trees, with the rabbits and the owls. No one would have found me there.

Getting Mother's permission for me to marry at sixteen was the hardest part for him to accomplish. I'm sure now she wishes she had never signed it. She raved about how she would kill herself first, but then she went in Father's Obsidian Study and when she came out, she did it, and I don't know why. She looked dazed. I haven't seen her as often as I wanted to for years. You know how she spent so much of her time with her position with the BC Agricultural Land Commission and didn't come for visits much.

But when she did, we would go camping together, and we'd have a great time, putting our blankets down on the ground, watching the stars, getting up with the birds at dawn. She must regret not spending more time with me when she had the chance. It's not like just anyone can come visit the Queen of the Order. At least once the Hadeskap College year is up, I can leave my post presiding over it for summer vacation and I can live with her. And even better, I can see my best friend again! Bounce bounce bounce. I miss you so much I can hardly stand it, my Jessica Blessica.

I want to tell you more in person this summer about how Dees and I have already kissed a whole lot. I wish I could get letters from you. I don't even know if you'll get these, maybe next month, but I want to send the letters up with the deliveryman after he brings the food, probably next time. If I could get letters from you, I'd ask if ladies are supposed to stick tongues out when men do, when we're French kissing. Is that a gross thing to do, like what just a man does? Do we pull our tongues far back? I just have no idea, and it's embarrassing. It makes me kiss him other places instead. I've been getting used to him a little more every day, and we cuddle, and call each other cute names, and sleep in late and read books together.

We had orange juice this morning. This month's food delivery just happened this morning, and the deliveryman's leaving now. I hear him talking to someone in the hallway. He seemed really nice, kind of nervous. I wanted to put my hand on his shoulder and tell him it's OK.

Oh, no, it sounds like a pig squealing or something. Or maybe it's the deliveryman. I've got to run see!

I'm back. I don't know what happened to the deliveryman. A man who has some high position in the Order that runs the school held me back and said it wasn't the scene for such a young woman. He seemed genuinely concerned. I liked having him touch me, too, such artistic hands, beautiful long fingers. Dees' hands are more... plebian? Is that the word? But I have to just be OK with those being the only man's hands to really touch me. You know what I mean.

Uncle Dees has been such a gentleman, waiting until the special ritual day to make love with me, but ooh, I never knew a man's body could be so smooth. I can't believe I'm not going to be a virgin after tonight. I'm going to be a real woman. It seems slightly gross, but I hear it grows on you. Hahaha.

I'm glad someone can be with him. That makes me glad it's me. Can you imagine? Who would voluntarily want to live down here without any sunshine ever, where you have to go into the Pomegranate Lodge and then the basement, and then keep going down hand-made elevator, and then stairs, and then go on some kind of thing that moves you across the giant underground facility before you get home. No wonder no one goes in and out very much. It's such a bother.

It sounds awful in the hall. It sounds like the deliveryman is dying! Poor man, I wish I knew what to do. There's nothing I can. It's just horrible sounding. It almost sounds like someone yelled "Hail Dees!" I know this sounds awful, but I was writing fast before trying to finish this letter before the delivery man went up, just in case. I'll just wait until the next month's delivery. I figured it would take too long to write what I wanted to get it off today. So much has happened since I saw you. I think it's been three weeks. I wasn't even engaged then. We never go so long without talking. Or purring, haha. knead, kneed. I miss playing with you, Jessica my Bestica.

And I miss my mother too. I know, she's not perfect, but I do. Can you give her a hug for me and tell her I'm looking forward to seeing her? But don't tell her about the deliveryman. It sounds like people yelling. I wonder if he did something really wrong and had to be killed. Everyone here sure would know how to do that, but I'd think they would do it fast, not draw it out like that. Or maybe it's a pig. Or both. Or maybe the people are squealing like pigs and the deliveryman is screaming. I think that might be it. Oh, Jessica, I'm shivering. I can't help crying right now, thinking about that poor man. I want to be up there with you, drawing pictures, and talking about boys in school and riding horses. I'd rather be doing chemistry than this. And you know how much I love chemistry.

And the strangest thing is, all the students down here that I've talked to so far have odd stories. One man pretends to the outside world he is dead. He's going to go back up after the school year is over, and work for my father's agency. It's like he won't exist anymore up there. I think he calls it "ghosting." No record, and with different fingerprints and even eye-scans, which sounds just horrendous. A lot of mutilation like that goes on here. It's kind of scary, sometimes, Jessica. I'm sorry, I said it. Father always taught me never to complain, to do what I'm told, to serve and expect life to be hard. The whole thing makes me really squeamish, though, just the same. I know that's like a girl. Queen Stephanie the Squeamish. That's how I'll go down in history.

Another student is in training to take over the identity of a boy who died, so he can investigate and infiltrate groups who do bad things. There are some classes in ways to kill people best. You know, like for people in the CSIS or police, special soldiers I think, stuff like that. When they go up, they're initiated into the Order higher up. I don't do anything with the school to speak of. I'm not sure what it is that's important about me being here, or why I'm Queen. It's fairy-taleish. I get to dress up in a better queen outfit for the initiation ritual tonight, I think. Still black, though, sigh.

Whoever heard of a pretty girl wearing black in a fairy tale? Even Cinderella just had dark clothes because of them being covered in soot. Only the bad ugly women wear black. I don't understand that part. I don't even tell lies, and I do what my family tells me to do. I got good grades in school. I guess I'm sort of bad because I'm not taking any classes now. I would, though, if there were any down here. I didn't want to drop out of school. Still, not having to do algebra and chemistry is really great. I get a lot more sleep than I did this time last year, not worrying about homework, and I don't have dreams about missing those tests, going to the wrong room at school. Can you imagine, going from that to this? Something about giving the students energy or something, I think. Kind of like a mascot, maybe the Homecoming Queen in a float. They root for the team or something.

The ritual is supposed to happen tonight. They're getting a room ready for it. It has wheat and pomegranates painted across the wall, is nice, really. There's a giant chair that's made out of wood that's carved in really interesting shapes. And, ooo, I don't know if I should tell you this. Don't tell anyone else, OK? Promise. We are supposed to take psilocybin. It grows down here. Who would have guessed, the mushroom that got our friend discharged from school and it's something all certain initiates do here that they get graded on. Some of them have already done it, or will later, but I think most of them do it at some point. It's supposed to help them get rid of their old selves, and open up to be made into what the school wants them to be. It helps them do their jobs better up top as new people.

It's supposed to be like dying and being reborn as what they have to be for the sake of the country. From what I understand it, most countries have this, not just ours. And the Order is in a whole lot of countries too, and sometimes I think it's even higher than the countries. Status-wise, you know. Some of the students here are women. The Order didn't used to let women in, because it just evolved that way over the centuries because women didn't do the job the men did. I think it's great there is some equality now. We're making progress.

The school, and especially the ritual tonight, is supposed to be really hard on them all. It's apparently traumatic and I think I'm supposed to comfort, or inspire them or something. Now, they're coming my way down the hall, and they're still yelling. They're screeching my name now, but it still sounds like pigs. I'm supposed to do something special to get ready. I'm about to find out. Amazingly loud. Like they're beating on my door with clubs! Their voices are scary! I'm going to pee my pants. Their voices are so violent. I don't know what to do, oh god, oh

The Biscuit Inspector

David Mathew

The Biscuit Inspector's official job title is Director of Quality Control, at Coronet Confectionaries – a manufacture-and-sales SME that employs sixty-two full-time staff in a factory and refrigerated warehouse complex on a trading estate in Worcestershire, and a dozen more sales representatives on patches throughout the UK and the Republic of Ireland. The Biscuit Inspector's role is to coordinate standards of output and team efficiency in a portfolio of comestibles that includes the Jelly Zinger, the Mayflair Mellow and the Orange Crackle. From time to time, when he can scrape his self-esteem up off the floor – and on the rare occasion that he is invited by anyone to elucidate his job description – he will joke that it is his responsibility to eat biscuits for a living and say that they are nice, at which point a further four million are produced and packaged. In fact, the Biscuit Inspector is now so high up on the company scaffold that he rarely has to put biscuit one to his thin lips anymore: he has a team to do this – a team of four people to eat biscuits all day, every day. Earning as he does, closer to eighty grand than seventy, the Biscuit Inspector feels hollow and unfulfilled in his role, and greets his half-yearly bonuses and incremental pay rises with a mixture of suspicion and dread.

Two years earlier, the Biscuit Inspector had decided to eschew the chauffeured drive to and from work and had started walking instead. When it rained he felt pleasantly guilty: bad weather was something that he ought to endure, for his salary. Although he left the house in the morning at 6.35 (after the Radio 4 news headlines), word had long since gone around the small community of local beggars and the homeless that at this time every day strolled a man who seemed hellbent on giving away pockets of change. The Biscuit Inspector tips every comer, young or old, not a princely sum per person, a pound or a two-pound coin, but for those prepared to ask nicely it is regular income. Nor is this the extent of the Biscuit Inspector's generosity. On a monthly basis, vast direct debits catapult chunks of his accumulated wealth in the directions of fifteen national charities, the better to ease his emotional burden with the notion that his contributions are helping the futures of blind children, rhinos and brain or heart surgeons, among many other donees. In addition, he gives money to a trio of cocaine salesmen on an ad hoc basis (before flushing his purchases down the toilet); and to a couple of favourite prostitutes, who listen to his self-deprecation in the knowledge of an eventual two hundred quid and the hope that on this one occasion he might even remove his trousers and give them something to work with.

The Biscuit Inspector is well aware that he is a boring man. He does not need to be told (he is never told, in fact): the truth is that he even bores himself. Although he has plenty of money to take up a hobby that might, in the fullness of time, colour in some of his soul's etiolation, the problem is that nothing grabs him. In the past he has enrolled on college courses in Film Studies and Radio Production (again, among others), on the lookout for a spark of recognition in his consciousness – a sign that this was what he'd been seeking all his life without knowing it – but found nothing apart from yet another certificate of completion. His one and only parachute jump ended well. He landed, inexpertly but safely, and rolled up the chute's fabric, then waddled to the side of the field, to the waiting off-road collection vehicle, a little chafed in his personal undercarriage by an unthought-through choice of beige underpants that morning, but otherwise healthy and unharmed. He reads novels and scores his verdict in a diary from years earlier that he did not fill in at the time. His scores are in the form of stars that he carefully draws with a heavy fountain pen that he bought in an antiques shop in Wiltshire on a whim, which he had hoped to use to compose his memoirs, before he recognised that he had nothing to say for his forty-four years on the planet.

Not that the Biscuit Inspector has failed to travel, of course! On the contrary, he has visited each of the continents at least twice, and even grew fond of a particular bar in Santiago for a while. At some point, towards the end of his thirties, the Biscuit Inspector realised a central irony that had escaped him up to then: that despite his work being in the Quality Control of sugary snacks, he was unable to quality control his own life or his own being. Not only did he adjudicate on the fate of biscuits, he was a biscuit himself! He was sweet and nice if taken quickly, but too much of him could make another person quite ill. Ordinarily immune to metaphor of any variety, this thought (which struck in him the aforementioned Chilean bar) clung to his brain with persistence. If everyone expected him to be a Jelly Zinger (for example), then perhaps on occasion he should at least attempt to be a Mayflair Mallow or an Orange Crackle.

'Stop thinking biscuits,' he murmured aloud to himself in the bar. Two male German holidaymakers at the next table – both of them a little the worse for wear after several rounds of coconut cocktails – believed the Biscuit Inspector to be talking to them, attempting to speak their language. The younger male was temporarily aggressive; the older forgiving and flirtatious. Accepting their invitation to their hotel room, and thereby desperately trying to be anti-biscuit, to be something new, the Biscuit Inspector was mildly disappointed that the German men had wanted nothing more from him than to hold the camera while they took turns at sodomising one another.

It was, however, a turning point of sorts. To the Biscuit Inspector it had at least become clear that if others found him pleasant in the short term and boring after any length of time, the trick would be to keep it brief. Whatever it was, keep it brief, and do not repeat yourself with the same person; make it once and once only.

On his return home to England, enjoying an almost-unknown fourth glass of champagne in Executive, the Biscuit Inspector removed his socks and waited for someone — air staff or civilian — to challenge him on the foot stink that he had been cultivating for the previous four days. Disappointed by the silence, he pulled a blanket over his lap and freed his penis. Feigning sleep felt delicious; it was the first time that he had done so, he believed, since the early days with his first and only wife, who had always desired conversation after their infrequent attempts at conception. Having established that he was asleep, his breathing an harmonic and hardy gurgle, the Biscuit Inspector, with caution as his byword, pulled gently at the edge of the blanket, an inch at a time, to the point where gravity took over and the blanket fell to the floor of the aisle. What the cabin crew saw, therefore, was a man in a tidy suit in Seat 5B, fast asleep and snoring, with his slim Johnson flat against the breached fly. Had the Biscuit Inspector been the kind of man to make notes, he would have recorded the cabin crew uttering such gobbets as: 'Well, *I'm* not touching it, Bobby!' or 'Someone should wake him up and tell him' or 'Why don't you put the blanket over his lap?' or 'Why don't *you* put the blanket over his lap?' But no one put the blanket over his lap, and the Biscuit Inspector feigned sleep for another half an hour, even searching for mental sexual imagery amongst his memories to make it grow (though this did not work). During this happy half-hour, the Biscuit Inspector, a man who had only sought imperfections in the familiar for twenty-one years, understood that the strange or not-welcome could be made ignorable or even invisible to people whose chief instinct was to want not to know.

Setting foot on the High Street on his return to work three days later, he was encouraged to acknowledge the approaching presence of a homeless man named Frank. The Biscuit Inspector had been giving Frank two or three pounds a week for the past fourteen months, and Frank's face was smiling and his long grey hair neatly combed. When he asked the Biscuit Inspector if he could spare any change, the Biscuit Inspector told him that there had been some alterations to the arrangement. At first, Frank assumed that this was a peculiar and out-of-character joke (perhaps his benefactor was ill); so when the Biscuit Inspector told him to follow, he did so. They walked away from the High Street, into an alley by the side of a vegetarian restaurant. At the end of the alley was a small courtyard, full of bins and a scattering of rat-traps. Your payment today is five pounds, Frank was told, provided you eat that; and the Biscuit Inspector pointed at a trap that had caught and all-but trepanned a small female rat of a battleship grey fur. Perfectly understandably (or so the Biscuit Inspector concluded), Frank showed hardy signs of perturbation and dismay. Nevertheless, the Biscuit Inspector was adamant about these new terms and conditions; indeed, he kept his voice calm and was close to ambling away when Frank made a step towards him and claimed that he could, as an alternative, simply take the money anyway, there being no cameras behind the restaurant to capture an act of violence for future evidence. The Biscuit Inspector merely smiled a smile that was every bit an enactment as the snoring on the plane had been, and he explained that if Frank so much as breathed too closely into his face, the Biscuit Inspector would go back to being driven to work every day, meaning that none of the other beggars would receive an additional penny from then on. Furthermore, the Biscuit Inspector would make it clear that Frank was the sole reason for the cessation of his generosity. You'll be shat on from now till you die, was the Biscuit Inspector's solemn, much-rehearsed (but again, feigned) conclusion.

The word circulated that the Biscuit Inspector had got stricter; that the gravy train had been derailed. To say that there was a sense of disbelief – that there existed the hope that the rumours were no more than a puzzling, Andy Kaufman-esque routine – was an understatement. On a daily basis, the Biscuit Inspector's regular beggars introduced new ways of being nice to their benefactor, assuming that his recent frugality was the result of being taken for granted. To a man and woman they were asked what they could do for the Biscuit Inspector in return. The automatic offer of a sexual favour (from some parties) was just as automatically dismissed as insufficient, especially given the amount of cash that they had already had off him over the previous two years.

It quickly become clear to the coterie that the options were simple. Either they mugged the Biscuit Inspector on a semi-regular basis, or they endeavoured to accommodate his modish demands for suitable compensation for his continuing financial handouts. Needless to say, the violence came first. The beating that the Biscuit Inspector received was sturdy and heartfelt; apparently it was also instantly regretted (it was not only Frank who had a tear in his eye as he aimed kicks at the Biscuit Inspector's head). As a result of the attack, the Biscuit Inspector was amused to note a shifting of emotional tone around him at work, when he emerged from hospital. A compassion; an atmosphere of empathy; with one of his team even going so far as to tell him, in a mutter, that it couldn't've happened to a wronger guy. The Biscuit Inspector gently thanked the colleague for his concern, but insisted that he was fine and that bruises and cuts healed of their own accord, in due course. Nor did the Biscuit Inspector change his walking plans for each working day; he did not so much as alter his route by one parallel street or a shortcut through the park that contained the war memorial.

After a few weeks of fiscal stalemate, during which despondent threats of further assaults were halfheartedly made, concentratedly rebuffed, and which came to nothing whatsoever, the word went around that if acts of self-debasement were what the Biscuit Inspector demanded, then perhaps they should get on with it and agree. In fact, some went so far as to state that they owed it to the man; and indeed, it was Frank himself who greeted the Biscuit Inspector one morning with his customary smile on his face and a dead grey rat in his left fist. Apologising for their earlier misunderstanding, Frank raised the rat's head to his own mouth and said *Bon appétit*.

During the months that followed, the Biscuit Inspector was treated to an ever-worsening display of pre-arranged defilement. Soon gleaning the man's peccadillo and his preference for watching them eat the customarily inedible, the coterie busied itself by imagining more and more disgusting things to put into its collective mouth or ingest. At work, the change in the Biscuit Inspector's demeanour had been noted, and not always positively or with enthusiasm. He was asked if he was having any personal difficulties, and these enquiries persist to this day, albeit less frequently than before. Each well-meant enquiry is met with an assurance that everything is well and that the Biscuit Inspector has never been more content in his home life. Enigmatically he might add that he no longer feels like a boring man. When he joins in on a tasting – it is rare but it happens – there is a gleam in his eye sometimes, as if he is thinking of something else.

A Dark Brass Pail

Connor de Bruler

In my dream, Willie Nelson asked me for a glass of wine. He was visiting my modest home (even in dreams I'm poor and complacent about it) to play poker with Emanuel, a co-worker of mine who was also my last remaining black friend ever since the doors of the university had permanently closed on me. My home was covered in flowers but, in the strange tunnel vision the dream afforded me, I couldn't see what kind of they were. I only remember an airbrushed, magenta blur covering the small cottage. Everyone and everything seeped into my dreams and, most of the time, I could wake up and recognize the people and the places my subconscious had sewn together, discombobulated, and otherwise edited for time and content. I asked Mr. Nelson if he wanted white or red wine.

"White," he said, without looking at me, tossing in a chip with an almost mechanical second nature; a suave indifference toward the pile in the middle of the table.

I went back to the old kitchenette, hoping there was more than just Bordeaux, bourbon, and beer in my dream fridge and felt my spirit lift when a cheap bottle of Pinot Gris had transported its way into my visions. All I had in the cupboard where plastic glasses but it didn't matter since they were shaped like traditional wine glasses, fancy ones. I brought the glass back to Willie Nelson feeling greatly accomplished. In most dreams reading a sign, or finding a train station, or dialing 911 often degenerated into cinematic drama marked by physical disfunction and failure.

He took one look at the drink and said, "Naw, you can leave the pitcher." So I left the glass on the poker table and went back to find a pitcher, but I had no pitcher. Instead, I cleaned out a brass watering pail, carefully scrubbing the edges in the sink, and poured the remainder of the bottle inside. Nelson accepted the vessel without question and I couldn't believe my success. The dream disintegrated into short bursts of unrelated ideas with the poker game as the focal point, the way dirty bath water circles a drain. I woke up and thought about the dream and all the things I knew existed in reality. I had a bottle of Pinot Gris that belonged to my girlfriend in the fridge. Emanuel, completely silent throughout the dream, happened to be the best holdem player I knew, and I had played exchange students from Macau. I wasn't sure why Willie Nelson was in my dream. I didn't listen to his music but I did work with a guy named Willy who sorted through rotten produce at the grocery store. In fact, the day before he talked a lot (too much actually) about lucid dreaming.

I stood up from the bed and parted the shabby curtains. Nothing but brittle forest and sawgrass appeared through my only window in the bottom-floor apartment. In the summer, I caught a glimpse of a black bear rummaging through the brambles, but that too might have been a dream.

I always took a walk before driving to work. The long-neglected sidewalk was chipping away beneath my feet and it worsened every year. Massive roots from the elms pushed up jagged slabs of concrete that were too high for some to stride across. The kudzu had repossessed a third of the pathway and, at the far end only a few yards from the tracks, the entire thing collapsed into ruin like broken pottery scattered in a field. The prevailing segments connected several low-income apartment complexes and ran parallel to the backyards of a cluster of ranch homes. My neighbors thought I was strange for taking walks, as if I was invading their privacy by choice. After my walk, I drove to work listening to the radio. Nelson Mandela had died the previous day. I can't remember if they said how. Old age, I think.

I worked at a health-food supermarket a few counties southward on the Bourbon Trail, between the Four Roses headquarters and the Wild Turkey distillery, in a flat town called Equus, where the gas stations were kept immaculate and horses outnumbered people. The drive was especially beautiful in the winter when long plains of perfect snow unsullied by red dirt and hoof prints and tractor tires blanketed the farmland in the early morning, lacing the edges of the salted interstate. At night, beneath the chalk-white bow of the crescent moon, shined the orbs of far-off suburban windows, and the sky was met with a faint blue dusting of hickory smoke. The horses were kept in the stalls most of the season, making brief, listless appearances at the edge of the fence, and the cows grew a scrappy coating of dog fur and behaved no different than in the summer, grazing in uneven clusters or sitting alone in the most precarious and forlorn corner of the entire pasture with their legs curled beneath their girth. The police cars were boxy, angular. Time halted. In the summer, the pastures turned radiant green and the muscle bound thoroughbreds triumphed against the daily commuters like me who passed the sides of the pastures like we were daring the horses to race. Some breeds could even outrun (if only for a short burst of victory) the reckless drivers from Ohio who traveled south for family reunions or whatever those disgusting people did with their time. Each season passed and I forgot what the other looked like and marveled at the same benchmarks and oddities. When I lived in the city, new buildings appeared. Old ones were demolished. Whole blocks had been eaten-up by pizza parlors, IPA pubs, and the hip new face of old yuppie gentrification. A fresh pink slip tucked into my coat (and most of the coats of my forgotten friends), I left the city still wondering where all the money had come from. It didn't matter because Equus, Bessemer, and Cantville never changed.

I took the same commute everyday and listened to the same radio station and pulled into the parking lot exactly ten minutes before my shift began. In the winter I walked inside, hung up my coat, and poured myself a complimentary cup of coffee. In the spring I did the same. In the summer I drank maté throughout the workday to stay energized. I drank bourbon when I got home and turned on the television. Four Roses for paycheck weeks. Early Times when it wasn't. Just two short swigs to promote a warmth in the stomach and head (then a few more for the rest of the limbs). My workday began with a long succession of "how are you doing?"s and "what's good?"s. I stepped through the deli kitchen to cut through to the grocery offices, running into every hairnet-wearing staff member I saw. The kitchen staff and deli attendants were the outlaws of the store; former chefs and restaurant workers from the upscale eateries of Chicago, Louisville, Indianapolis, and Knoxville who had either retired or abandoned the frantic pace of the to-order schedule for the lazy world of batch cooking for a health food store's cafeteria. I bought my weed from the kitchen people. There was one cook I remember in particular. Her name was Azalea. She was a forty-two-year-old white Jamaican women who only stood five-feet tall in heels and weighed 120 pounds soaking wet. She had lived in Kentucky since her adolescence if not childhood and her accent was a mix of Patois and a terse Kentucky drawl. I talked to Azalea first even before Emanuel, who the store (or perhaps even Emanuel himself) had chosen to call E-man, or the manager, Todd, a short Polish kid from Florida, or Tommy, a tall dark guy from the meat department who had been a professional bluegrass musician and trucker across Appalachia in another life, or willy in produce who always had something pithy up his sleeve and reeked of sweet Kentucky weed. Azalea was always the one I spoke to first and usually last. Her face, which was still by most standards objectively beautiful, displayed a distinctive wear-and-tear through dark creases in her subtly graying teeth and wrinkles in her face that tallied a few months lost to the hillbilly cocaine. She kept her hair wrapped in two Indian braids and matted down the rest of her scalp with a knitted cap. I remember a story she had told Emanuel in the cold, dry air of the stocking room, a price gun in her hand.

"The doghouse," she said. "I'm about to go home to my doghouse."

"How come you in the doghouse?"

"I pissed him off again."

"Who you piss off?"

"Him."

"Him?"

"Okay, so I got a sense of humor that's rough round the edges. I know this. You know this."

"I heard that. What's going on with ya?"

"You know my husband used to be an alcoholic, right? I mean, him used to be a big mahn. But he just lost like thrity pounds An I think, he's alright with him weight, right? So we're jokin', just havin' a laugh. He play'd a prank on me for Valentines Day. He say, 'I done got you a gift.' Shows me a computer page for a swingers website. I laugh. He laughs. Den he say, 'So for the day I could watch you screwin' a forty-year-old sack of flab. How's that sound?' I say, 'You want me to put a mirror above our bed?' Then he get all incredulous about it. I tell him sorry, but he's still angry."

"You gotta make a gesture girl."

"All yesterday I'm gesturin'."

There were rumors her husband still beat her from time to time. I never saw Azalea with a black eye or bruises. I'm not sure what her husband did for living, but they had enough money to take a trip to Jamaica each winter. She'd disappear around February when the sky turned to smudges of coal ash. She would show me the pictures of the withered Kingston garrisons and the

brightly painted storefronts, the clear ocean and the crowded ma-
rinas. She had a bottle of Guinness in most of the pictures, the
good kind with the yellow label that must have still tasted like
something unlike the canned shit we import in the U.S. that's
gone flat and tastes like aluminum. She looked forward to those
February trips and said she was going back upon the rock. Jamaica
was the rock. I would picture her lying on the beach in a white
bikini, her strange, nimble body an oddity regardless of her surroundings, smoking a thick blunt. She smoked marijuana with
the frequency of cigarettes, at least as far as I could tell in the
uncomfortable atmosphere of the modern work environment. She
was unfazed by the most potent strands She bragged about smoking white-window in Zig-zag wrap. Despite her candid nature,
she never admitted to her brief love affair with methanphetamine.

I drove Azalea home once. Her car had broken down in the parking lot and Tommy, the only guy with jumper cables, had gone home
for the evening. She would have asked Emanuel for a ride but, as I had
suspected sadly, women didn't trust him alone. I think she felt safer
with me. I'm a timid guy. I'm a nice guy. I was already late when she
asked and her ranch home wasn't very far. We drove in the darkness for
awhile, talking about other times we were in similar situations the way
people do when they have nothing better to talk about. We got off the
freeway and she told me to head down a long gravel road that passed
by a trailer park I had seen on the news a few times because so much
meth was cooked and sold there. Azalea said something about her best
friend Julia living out there, and I seemed to recall a story she had told
me about her. Julia worked as a masseuse in Cantville.

"Forty bucks for an hour-long session ain't bad," she said.
"Specially not on a Saturday evening. Yeah, I'm headed out that
way now. Gonna give her a nice tip for Christmas. She's excellent.
Workin' for a new place now."

"A masseuse must be a good friend to have," I told her,
stocking alkaline waters for Iceland.

"Oh, you bet. Got these three rowdy kids. One of 'em's a screamin' toddler. We hang out in her trailer a lot. So, the toddler comes up to us screamin'. She takes one touch on the shoulder, starts wigglin' her thumb. The kid drops to the floor asleep like this..." She fell to the floor to corroborate her story. "She says, 'Damn, I'm good.' I say, 'You done knocked out your lil' pickney, geeyal!'"

We passed the trailer park and she muttered something else about Julia, then she told me to make a left at a scarecrow that almost made me jump in my seat. I looked like a demented hobo in the eerie glow of my headlights. The branch protruding from its sleeve could have been a rusted bread knife.

Azalea's home was big and dark. Only one light was on in the kitchen. I could smell the smoke from the chimney in the car. I was envisioning her husband pulling her from my car with a bottle of whiskey in his hand, but the entire home appeared derelict with the exception of the single kitchen light through which I could see a fridge decorated with photos and a wood-paneled hallway. She thanked me for the ride, gave me some cursory instructions on getting back and that was it.

That had been months before I found out she was fired. I was shocked when I found out the day after my dream. Tommy gossiped with me in the meat locker.

"Apparently, one of the managers caught her taking a smoke break"–Tommy lifted his fingers to form quotation marks– "in her car before work."

"Aw, shit!" I said. "She got caught with weed?"

"No, it was a circular glass pipe."

"Jesus."

"Yeah," He paused. "She's got some issues."

I never saw her again.

I worked a long day and drove home listening to a different radio station. The road was always empty at night except for a few trucks and wayward travelers heading up to Louisville or Indiana. I got home around 9: 40

pm. My headlights nearly touched my front door. I kept my keys in my hand when I got out of the car, but immediately noticed a slight indention around the perimeter of the door that told me it wasn't locked. My girlfriend was inside. She had a key to my place and seldom locked the door when she knew I'd be home so soon. I walked in and locked the door behind me She was already on my couch in her pajamas.

"Hey, babe."

"Hey," I said.

"How was your day?"

I shrugged and said, "I had a weird dream just before I woke up."

"What about?"

"Hang-gliding."

"Bullshit."

I walked the three paces to the kitchenette.

"Hey, can I have a glass of wine?"

"Sure."

I poured myself two-fingers of bourbon and searched the cupboards for the glasses. I couldn't seem to find any since I never put anything back in the same place when I unload the dishwasher. I looked beneath the sink and found a dusty brass pail I once used for decoration in my old loft apartment, back when I lived in the city. It was the exact pitcher I gave to Willie Nelson. I ended up pouring my girlfriend her wine in a coffee mug. She took it and laughed, asking me if my other glasses were dirty. I told her it might be easier if I just left her a pitcher of wine. She laughed and lit a cigarette. I told her Azalea got fired and she nodded. I told her it was meth. She nodded again and tapped her ash into the crystal tray and told me to forget about it. We watched television for an hour or two and, when the news finally eclipsed the comedy shows, slumped along to the bedroom. I lay in bed thinking about vessels, listening to her breath in her sleep when I remembered the flowers in my dream home. The bushels of magenta blurred from my vision were azaleas. They had to be.

Three Days

E. M. Stormo

A night bird sat on a chain link. It wasn't a singer. It sat snug in a diamond, doing nothing. The fluorescence shined it out for the two men walking by, one tall, one short, both skinny with fat bellies. The tall-fat man, Henry, delighted in attacking the nightlife. He flicked a rock at the bird and knocked it off the fence. Then he picked it up and drank from it with one hand. "None sweeter than a bird's kiss," he said, smacking his lips. Henry drank again and hurled the bird over the twenty foot fence where it disappeared into the dark woods. The short-fat man, Abe, was disgusted by his companion's antics, but said nothing. He was busy making a mental map of the area. Every time Abe stopped to draw in new details, Henry flicked another rock, killed another bird, and drank from it. Other less traveled paths snaked around them, all of it lit up like a neural network, which is why they call this place "the Brain." From above, it looked like a giant electrical brain, but it was just one of the three local television stations.

Henry, like Abe, was from the demoralized post-war generation, living a limbo life on a stateless sliver of land called the Corridor, where the conventions of the civilized world didn't always apply. After the bombings of the First Wave, the soldiers were starved, the women raped, and the men beaten and forced to watch. Their generation were often missing something: eyes, legs, and ears, but they all lacked their humanity, as could be seen in their facial expressions: permanently misshapen. No matter how hard they tried to smile politely, their faces always slid back into despair. So if Geneva had no say here, then the usual ethics need not concern the young men who survived the Second Wave. Personalities like Henry were all too common: animal abusers and sexual deviants.

Abe might have become one himself, were it not for his family, a rare opportunity here. Female flight during the previous years had taken nearly seventy percent of women across the river to the east or the mountains to the west, whether willingly going with their captors or shamed into leaving by their families. The male populations outnumbered the females ten-to-one. Abe married the only girl he knew from his town, although she could neither tend house nor return his love. Whenever they fought, he retreated to the comfort of his vivid imagination. Anywhere else, such a rich mental space would be known as a mind palace, but there were no palaces here. Abe likened his mind to a dirt basement, like the shelter underneath his apartment building. The shelter was empty except for some beans and vermin, but in his mental basement, there was enough room to spread out his living map in three dimensions. The homeland stood up like a skinny-fat man. At the top, there was the Brain glowing in the woods. The man's back laid against the mountains as he peed a holy river.

Despite not existing as a real country, there were plenty of detailed maps of the area, physical and electronic. But it was Abe's habit to memorize the entire lay of the land himself, out of a perfectly reasonable paranoia; he would use his mental map if and when they ever shut the power off again.

Abe closed his eyes and saw the blacktop was approaching in a half-mile. The black trees were so thick around them it kept out the field lights entirely, and the other pat lights shone dimly.

Henry drank some more birds. He wasn't starving as there was plenty of grain and succulents to give them both fat guts.

Thousands of swollen bellies had convinced international authorities of widespread famine in the area, but it was the opposite. There was practically zero work or activity of any kind among the population; they had grown fat doing nothing. The local government started an initiative to convert old factory sites into public parks. During the massive pillaging of the Second Wave, the glassworks and steel mills were dismantled piece by piece. What remained when the new power station was being built was a rubble footprint of a thousand square feet cemented down in the middle of the woods. These paths had been walked on for centuries, but the fencing and lights were a modern security measure, mostly to protect the foreign workers. Blacks owned these woods, and they were much meaner than the Browns who scrounged openly in the cities. Both Blacks and Browns were illegal to hunt down, a redundant law for the locals religiously favored bears, as the Indians do their cows, and whether nasty or apathetic, Blacks and Browns belonged to a protected species. Even Henry wouldn't dream of harming a bear, although he might delight in scaring them off. Like his ancestors, Henry believed in blood magic, at least unconsciously; he could taste the bird's life-force filling him up. He drank from another and offered some to his companion, but Abe refused. He sucked a kiss loudly and told Abe, "It's not just blood, but everything else in one go."

Evidence of the occupations remained where diamond fence turned to square fence. This section of the fence also had razor wire on top. When Henry threw his last bird over it got stuck in the wire. Abe told Henry, "Keep away from the fences." He saw on his map, the Blacks like to congregate here. That kind of detail wouldn't be on anything but a living mental map.

When they reached the clearing, it was obvious the public initiative had funneled most of the money into the government official's pockets. The old glassworks was a black rectangle. They paved it with asphalt and painted a baseball diamond. These wasteful projects were called "theatres." From above, it looked like a movie screen.

And yet, twenty or so men sat around like an old painting under the fluorescence. It was only cool enough to sit at night. They drank in a circle and passed around a couple jugs of wine. Elijah had his guitar and played folk songs from the First Wave. Other men played cards, drank coffee, or just laid down on the black ground, and in the background, Joshua bounced a ball on his knee, trying to start a game. Abe closed his eyes to take a snapshot of the scene, which Henry did his best to fit into, but found himself hanging by the fence.

Abe came over to recruit Henry for the game. He stood against the chain, smoking and drinking the last sips from one of the wine jugs. An animal whimpered from the black trees.

"It's a Brown," said Henry.

"Come on. Let's play," said Abe.

"I don't."

"You threw those birds pretty high."

"Fine." Henry flicked his cigarette through the fence hole. "They will probably bomb us in the middle of the game."

"I hope not," said Abe as if it needed to be said.

The men split into two teams and for an hour their spirits lifted. For the family men, it was good to get away. For everyone else, it was nice to bond over something other than their shared oppression. Henry and Abe ended up on the same team. Abe noticed Henry took it more seriously than anyone. All of the men were skinny with fat bellies, but they could still run and pass with the dexterity of a hardened race. Growing up among bombings and beheadings can make men fit for almost anything, despite the toxins in the rivers and air intended to effeminize them. They were drunk enough they didn't care and lost track of the score. It was a good time until the lights went out.

A bear growled. Elijah screamed. He instantly went mad in the darkness. "It was a Black," said Henry, but that didn't help anyone, although Abe believed him to be mildly prophetic. They looked up to the sky, expecting the bombs to drop any moment. There had to be a Third Wave, and yet they always thought of themselves as the Third Wave. First, the lights go out and then the planes come, either over the river or the mountain. Everyone hesitated at first, not because they were in shock, but because they half-welcomed a merciful if not belated death. The bombs took too long however, and they snapped to attention, if only to go die at home.

Abe led them through the woods in the dark. His mental map came in handy as they jogged back to the Brain. They heard someone coming towards them, heavily breathing.

"Who's that?" asked Joshua.

The breathing got closer. The men picked up rocks.

"We'll strike you down!" he called out.

A man appeared, but nobody threw anything. He was a reporter who fled from the TV station. He was lost running around the woods. "I got away from them," he said when he caught his breath.

"Who was it?" asked Joshua. "From the mountain, or the river?"

"From the mountain," said the man, and everyone groaned. He wept and nobody questioned him further. He was young and commuted from the city. The terror would come to them too, but it would be psychological in nature.

That's when they heard it: women screaming. The women who screamed for three days. They screamed from the woods. They screamed from the villages and the city. They screamed from every house and every station. Everywhere in the stateless corridor, the women's screams could be heard.

At first, it wasn't clear where the women were, for they seemed to be everywhere in the woods. Even the bears were spooked by it. Henry was the first to figure it out. "It's coming from the station." The station itself seemed to be screaming. The Brain was smothered in women's screams as of an alien thought implanted into a man's head, but this wasn't the psychotronic warfare from the Second Wave. There was nothing electromagnet-ic or magical; the technology was old-school enough that it could work in their homes.

The men reached a checkpoint in Abe's mind; it was also where Henry had killed a bird. They were divided on what to do next: go to the station or back to the village.

"We should open the fences and let the Blacks out," said Henry. They considered it for a second, but they knew the soldiers were armed and would gun down the bears before they lost any men.

"Blacks are sacred," said Elijah, as they were all aware, and nobody would dream of doing them harm. Even killing one in self-defense was wrong.

They approached the station; the lights were on. Joshua climbed the fence to get a better look. He could see the building and a small army outside. He climbed back down slowly, careful not to rattle the chain.

"What did you see?" someone yelled up at him.

He jumped down and put his hand over the man's mouth. "Let's go," he whispered. His face had gone fluorescent.

Once they got out of the woods, the men collapsed to their knees. This was more exercise than they were used to, especially after the game. The screaming was less, but now it could be heard miles away in the direction of their village, unnatural screams amplified. Abe used his mental map of the skinny man to find shortcuts. In the heart of the man was the town where Abe and Henry lived, but in the bowels of the man there were was a city, as modern as any, where the local government leaders made their deals to sell out the Corridor.

Abe remembered a shortcut that would temporarily put them on state land, but under the circumstances they had to risk it. The river flowed nearby. Their ancestors bathed in it for centu-ries, but this was impossible now as it existed beyond a military checkpoint. Elijah hummed an old wave song about uniting the people, commonly by one race in opposition to the foreign enemy, but such an idea was scoffed at by today's youth, and Elijah himself knew it was unrealistic.

They returned to the village around dusk. Joshua left them at his blacked-out building. Half of the village was dark, but Abe's half still had electricity and that's where the last screams led them. It wasn't only women screaming, but also the light grunting of men.

Abe left them at his building which was only a couple buildings away from where Henry lived. They didn't say anything as they parted but looked at each for a second, their faces contorted to the same awful expression.

Abe ran up two flights of stairs to his apartment. He tuned out the screams, or they were covered in static. Neighbors stood outside, but nobody said anything. The doors were open in some of the apartments and he could see everyone staring at their TVs, although he couldn't see what was on the TV, but they were watching the same thing. He struggled with his keys in the lock, until his wife Elizabeth cracked open the door. She wasn't screaming.

"Who is it?" she asked.

"It's me," said Abe. "Open the door."

"Okay," she creaked the door back, "but you weren't here."

It was their women. On the TV. The ones from the river were known for mass rapings during the First Wave. But these were their women. The ones from the mountain. They had filmed their women screaming like he had never heard a woman scream before. It was their women, but also their men. His children stared at it. He changed the channel between the other three stations to find the same thing. He flicked the switch off on the TV and the screaming stopped.

"Why didn't you just turn it off?" Abe asked his family.

"We tried to change the channel," said Abe. Jr., "It's on all of them."

"We couldn't do anything," said his eldest, Isaac. "It just happened to us."

"Why not turn it off?" he repeated.

"We tried," said Elizabeth. "At first, it was only clips. And then, this."

"Why not turn it off?" he yelled.

His youngest, Abigail began to cry as if she now understood what she had been watching.

"It was so loud," said Abe.

"No, it wasn't," said Elizabeth.

"We could hear them screaming from the woods!"

"They're enjoying it," she said.

He closed his eyes and found himself on the other side of the world in unmapped and unoccupied territory. It was a bad habit his family knew well; how he loved to exist in the darkness of his own mind more than anywhere else. She came to him that night anyway, and he allowed her on top of him. Hundreds of babies were conceived in the days of the terror programming, a generation they officially called the Third Wave.

The TVs in Henry's apartment received amazing reception. He stayed up watching it all night and turned it off in the afternoon of the next day, but then turned it back on again later that afternoon, and watched another night's worth until he couldn't watch it anymore but forced himself to anyway, glued to the television for three days straight until mercifully, it shut itself off.

"No, no, no," his grandfather Josiah groaned from the bedroom. Henry forgot he lived with someone. After staying up three days, Henry wanted to drown in the river or get lost in the mountains; let a bear drink him. Josiah kicked open his bedroom door. He was spry for his age, but he looked unusually fresh. He stepped over Henry to grab his pack of cigarettes.

"Are you dead?" asked Josiah.

"Yea," said Henry.

"Good."

His grandfather was a soldier from the First Wave, back when they actually had an army. After he was captured, he was cut by the enemy and sent home half a man, so he made a relic of his skin and stored it in a jar on his bookshelf. He examined it every day to remind himself of his hatred for the mountain itself and the river itself which were his true and natural enemies. Henry always assumed he was impotent before he stepped out of his room, practically giddy.

"Let's throw some rocks today," said Josiah.

"Yea, Grandpa," said Henry, and like a dog shrugs off water, he picked himself off his spot on the floor.

Ripe

Connye Griffin

"Hey, there, Justin."

I looked across the chrome engine of that '69 Charger, Pa's birthday gift to me. It'd be ready to drive come my next birthday—just 24 more days.

"Hey, Dani."

"What time ya get off?"

"We gotta plenty ta do. He don't have no set time. Now git!"

I watched her to see how she took Pa's meanness. She was just fine, smilin', twistin' apiece of that luscious strawberry hair with one hand while t'other traced the low scoop of her tight tee. She watched me back, then turned ripe hips full round so I could see 'em real good afore she swayed 'em side ta side on her way back to her truck. She let one leg hang in the air a bit 'fore she tucked it inside and tugged on them cut-offs, givin' me plenty of time to eye that leg, neon orange peep toes, a thin gold chain round a tiny ankle, on up to her tight round thigh against soft brown leather. She watched me watch her and smiled. I knew she couldn't see how rock-hard she'd made me—that Dodge stood between her and me, but her eyes told me to "Come on" and I almost did—until I caught sight of Pa. Formidable.

"You ain't ripe yet, Boy," Pa warned me later. "It's comin'; they're comin' but you wait 'til your next birthday. Those womin'll stand in line, and you kin have 'em all if'n you jest wait."

I knew what Pa had in mind, and it wasn't what I had in mind. I wanted to strip them girls naked and find the heart of that musky scent. I wanted to taste 'em. I had no mind to drag 'em out back into the woods just to make 'em scream. I sure didn't plan to run 'em off like he did ever' month. They'd come knockin' like flies on shit and he'd choose one. I'd hear him ruttin' on her and she'd start moanin' low then higher until she couldn't hit another note, then nothin'. Not another sound. Just leaves rustlin', fadin' deeper in them woods out back. Pa'd come on back, lookin' smug, struttin' like a Rhode Island Red. Sometime in the night, I'd hear that old gal's car start up, but she'd never be back. One time with Pa ruined 'em. I don't know what he done, but he ruined 'em.

One evenin' the sheriff come callin'.

"Simmons, come on out now. I gotta speak to you."

Pa looked real mean, but he went, and I could hear 'em.

"Folks say the last time anyone saw Peggy Jean was on her way out here. Did she come out here, Simmons?"

"I ain't seen her."

"You haven't seen her today or last week."

"I reckon the last time was couple months ago when she needed a new fan belt on that Chevy. I changed it out for her—had the car half day."

"She never drove out here to your place?"

"Naw—why?"

"You tell me. Folks say quite a few women come callin' out here."

"They don't stop here, Sheriff. They must be meetin' up out in those woods, but they ain't here."

"Can I look around your place, Simmons? Come back tomorrow and look around?"

Pa didn't like it. He got all quiet and made the sheriff wish he'd brought back-up along with him. Pa could be fierce when he took a mind to be. Anyone who'd ever questioned him at the shop learned not to. They'd settle up with Pa, or they'd be walkin' to work 'til they did. Word got 'round so people'd pay, but Pa wasn't chargin' too much, and he did what he said he'd do. Some folks just try to feel big by makin' workin' guys feel small. Pa was plenty big and set that type man right back on the ground.

Finally, Pa said, "You can come back and take a look, Sheriff, butcha won't find nothin'. They ain't been out here."

"I'll be back tomorrow then. Good night."

Pa didn't say nothin' when I stepped out the door, stood beside him. That girl'd been here just two weeks ago, but I knew better than to offer my notions and I sure knew not to ask Pa why he'd said he hadn't seen her. We just stood, watching until the spot of red taillight couldn't be seen no more.

Life was pretty good after Pa had him a gal. He still had plenty a vinegar but there was some honey, too. He'd close up the shop in town at four instead of hangin' round 'til dark a night. We'd go home, sometimes hunt up some rabbit 'fore supper. Pa could be real quiet—so quiet he'd snatch that rabbit mid-jump. Sometimes I thought that rabbit come right to him.

Afterward, we'd talk about nothin' while Pa sliced the neck and let the blood pour into a pan. Then he'd stripped the pelt, leaving the carcass smooth and shiny. He'd hold it real still, resting in his palms, pettin' it with his thumbs, his eyes closed in reverie, just like another person'd pet the soft fur. Seein' him like that put me in mind of someone prayin'—like what those Cajun folks do before they kill a pig at an old-fashioned *boucherie*. And just like them, next he'd carve that rabbit and cut the meat off the bone. He threw the guts into the blood and set it on the fire to stew while he sliced the meat real thin and laid it out in the oven to dry out for out jerky. I'd stretch the pelt between four sticks to dry. Once it was free of rot and varmints, we'd stitch it along one side or t'other of the blankets we slept under in the winter.

Other nights, those nights soon after them girls had paid him a visit, Pa'd stoke up the brick oven outside, and we'd barbeque a mess a ribs, let a roast smoke all night. This was the only kind a cookin' Pa did. He had his own special rub that made the meat salty and sweet all in the same bite. We'd feast for nigh two weeks on that meat, but when it and the rabbits ran out, we ate nothin' but beans. I loved them fresh meat nights. They always made me feel strong.

Pa'd turned real sour not long after them nights. He'd stay busy down to the shop, one gal or 'nother tryin' to rub up on him. I knew to keep to the shadows, stay out a sight. Pa needed them womin, but he never went after one. They just come to him. He liked the ones that didn't have nobody—not kinfolk in the hills, nary a brother or a cousin anywhere—made 'em real eager, needy like. 'Cept Peggy Jean. He didn't find out about her kin down Alabama askin' after her 'til she'd made her visit. Her folks sent the Sheriff out our way when they couldn't find her, and in no time, that Sheriff turned up Peggy's car in a deep, dark coal pit some three miles away. More sniffin' 'round and more questions and one night, he come for Pa.

I didn't say nothin' and I didn't try to stop the Sheriff. I knew what to do. Pa saw the day when I'd need to know. On his way out the door, Pa said, real quiet, just to me, "Now, boy. Go."

So I did. I went right to the shop in town first. Under the drawer in our old brass till was a yellow tear of paper folded 'round some money—a lot a money. On the paper, Pa wrote all neat-like, "Put the camper top on the pickup and go. Drive the back roads—nothin' wider than a lane or two. Go deep into the woods and stay there. Don't worry 'bout nothin'. They'll come to you. They ain't got a choice. Don't stay in one spot too long. You're ripe now, boy."

I was gone before the sun come up, drove all day and into the next night afore I turned up an old mine road and wedged the truck way back off the road in under some trees. I slept through 'til the next night, my birthday, and woke up wishin' Pa was there to tell me what I was s'posed to do now that I was ripe. I woke up hungry, too, hungrier than I ever remember bein'. I kicked myself for not grabbin' some jerky on my way out the door. Then I heard somethin' or someone on the road some thirty yards yonder with steps light like a woman's, and I started hopin' she'd have some food on her, but when she come into sight, she had nothin' but herself and she come, pullin' off her tight tee, unzippin' short khaki cut-offs, her soft skin luminous against the dark night.

"Hey, there."

"Hey, there, yourself."

"I'm here for you."

"I know ya are," and I did, too. Pa said to wait 'til my birthday, and I had, but I didn't have to wait no more. Pa said they'd come to me, and here she lyin' down naked on leaves and twigs like there was nothin' that might crawl 'cross her or bite her in the ass. She wasn't afraid at all.

I stood over her, just admirin' her shape, round and full in all the right places. I put one knee on each side of those soft, ripe hips and knit my hands in hers, sweeping them in mine until they were over her head, my chest against her mouth where she kissed me and started a low moan deep in her throat while her hips rose to meet mine. With one hand holding her arms pinned, I let the fingertips of my other hand tickle along her inner arm, around each nipple, and down her belly to the navel. I unzipped my jeans and pulled myself free. I knew just what to do, and I knew as sure as if I'd been standin' watchin' him all those years just what Pa'd done with those womin.

Cupping both hands under her shoulders, I lifted her up and felt her heart thunder as she pulled herself closer, tighter against me. I pressed my lips against the pump, pump, pump at her neck, and she tilted her head, opening more of her neck to me. She hit a high note when I bit down hard, pulling flesh and muscle and veins in one big bite. As I pulled back to chew the salty, bloody, sweet flesh, I saw her eyes open real wide, lookin' at somethin' far off over my shoulder, seein' what she'd come for—to feed me, to sate me. I let her body fold back into the earth, swallowed, and took another mouthful at her breast. She'd smelled me from far off. She was fresh meat right off the bone, born for my kind.

After I chewed real good and picked the meat from between my teeth with a sturdy twig, I shoved her under the pickup. She'd be there—nice and ripe—in the mornin' so I could set to work then, cuttin' out roasts and ribs, snackin' between slices. I'd unload the roaster and spend the day stockin' up, then I'd move on, leaving her bones to be carried off by Turkey Buzzards and coyotes. They'd gnaw and scatter them bones for me. Winter'd bleach 'em pure again.

Too bad Pa hadn't let 'em walk right in instead of drivin'. Maybe it was me that made him settle. I'd have to be sure not to make a me cuz now I knew: cars and kin'll getcha. I'll just let 'em walk right in and move on down the road when I'm spent.

A Room At The Marriott In Times Square

Kenneth Levine

I will, then won't, and change my mind two more times before I finally pick a *Village Voice* out of a street-side bin, return to my room at the Marriott, and make the calls. By 12:15 A.M., an hour and twenty minutes later, part of me wants to cancel, but a more insistent part demands I don't. It's probably too late anyway; any second I expect her to knock on the door. I look out the fortieth floor window at Times Square crowds bustling beneath neon illumination in mockery of the diurnal cycle. Perhaps she's among the throng.

While I wait for her to arrive, I think about the three day seminar, *Tax Planning for Domestic & Foreign Partnerships, LLCs, Joint Ventures & Other Strategic Alliances*, I'm here to attend. I've promised myself this time I'll be present at each session, the first of which begins tomorrow morning, instead of behaving as if I'm on vacation. I need to earn continuing legal education credits.

At 12:30 A.M. I hear three taps, each softer than the one before. I peer through the peep hole at the top of a head of long, dark hair. When I open the door, a woman looks at me and says, "I'm Esperanza. Are you Steve?"

I nod and motion her into the room, while I look her over. She's about thirty-five, and because she's a head shorter than me, no more than five feet four. Her face is rectangular, but her cheeks are round. She's wearing a black leotard that shows off breasts that are smallish, but still a handful, and a disappointing flabby paunch, and jeans so tight her thick, round ass looks like it's made of denim. She holds a satchel in her hand.

Esperanza is not what I desire. She's another in a lifetime of compromises: becoming a lawyer to please my parents, marrying to not be alone, and now Esperanza instead of an exotic woman from India with dark, luxurious pubic hair like the women in the movie, *The Kuma Sutra*, who I solicited from the escort services or my backup request for a big-breasted black woman. The fourth service said, "We have no women from India. We'll have a black one available tomorrow. But there's a well-rounded, white, Hispanic woman with big breasts men have been happy with during her three weeks with us. Her name is Esperanza." So much for truth in advertising.

I remove ten twenty dollar bills from my wallet and wave them through the air like a fan as I place them on the nightstand. Staring at me, Esperanza says, "You're a cop."

Surprised by her accusation, I say, "I'm not," with so much uncertainty even I'm not convinced.

Esperanza says, "I have to use the bathroom." She backs away and disappears behind its closed door. I hear her speak: "It's Esperanza," and after a pause, "I think he's a cop," followed by silence, then, "He put the money on the nightstand," more silence, "You're sure?" another pause, and, "Okay." Then the toilet flushes and water flows from the sink's faucet. I wait for her to return, wondering if I followed the wrong protocol. The first time I paid an escort, she said, "No honey. You don't hand it to me. You put it over there and maybe I'll take it and maybe I won't." And afterward she took it. I've seen enough *Law and Order* episodes to know prostitutes worry as much about a police sting as I worry about being arrested, beaten, or blackmailed, but I'm a tax attorney, not a criminal lawyer, and I don't remember anything about what my law school professor said about entrapment thirty-seven years ago.

Esperanza emerges in a black negligee with the bag in hand. She places it on the desk, sits on the bed, and says, "Can you make me a drink?"

"I don't have anything," I say, without thinking this is the Marriott and there must be a mini-bar with little bottles of alcohol, and then when I do think it, at two hundred dollars an hour for her time, I don't want to spend any of it making drinks that won't be reimbursed by my firm.

Esperanza lies on her side, facing me, with her elbow spearing the bed and her head resting on her hand. She says, "Why don't you take off your clothes and join me?"

I undress, and my penis, which is under the magic spell of fifty milligrams of Viagra, points heavenward. I climb into bed beside Esperanza, and she immediately grabs my privates, coaxing from the well of my testicles the tsunami of shame and guilt I felt the other times I was with prostitutes.

I inhale deeply, trying to clear my head. I'm not the sort of person who frequents hookers. I'm too smart and good looking, too advantaged, too everything. That's what degenerates, losers and miscreants, the perverted and sick, the not-me's do. My father would never be here, nor my brothers, but here I am. Again. I tell myself I have grounds for my behavior. After my wife is aroused, she touches my penis for a couple of minutes, we have intercourse for about ten, and she says, "It hurts. Finish yourself." I should divorce her, but won't for the reasons I married her: I had nowhere and no one to go to. I married my wife, at whose apartment I lived, after she issued the ultimatum: "Marry me or move out," because I heard Julia, the girlfriend I had when I was in law school and the only woman I've loved, was married and pregnant. I'm stuck. Stuck in the past. Stuck in my marriage. Stuck in me.

Esperanza tightens her grip on my penis and massages my shame away. I reach under the top of her negligee, and as I cup her right breast, then the other, discovering their weightlessness, my guilt is replaced by the adventurousness of an explorer. "I want to see all of you," I say. I scrunch a swathe of the fabric and pull it away from her bosom. "Take it off."

Esperanza slips the negligee over her head and discards it on a chair. She lies on her back, and I place my hand below her neck and glide it to her right breast, her left, then straight down the center of her body past her navel to the top of her panties. As I slide my fingers beneath the elastic and over a tuft of hair and into her core, she takes a quick, deep breath, which inflates her bosom, and becomes as stiff as a board.

I'm bewildered by Esperanza's discomfort, and as I remove my fingers, decide three weeks as a prostitute should have been sufficient for her to become accustomed to the touch of a customer. Prostitutes are supposed to pretend they like what they're doing. That's their job. I don't like my job, but I do it, and when I'm with a client I act as if I like it, although perhaps, like Esperanza, I'm not a good enough actor and that's why the partners in my law firm choose to not make me a partner, instead offering the consolatory remark: "It was a close vote." I remember a woman I dated when I was a college student. We were on my bed, her top was off and her jeans were open and unzipped, and I slipped my hand down her panties. I withdrew it when she froze, and we never shared another physical intimacy. But this isn't Amy Guilder; it's Esperanza, and I'm paying for her services.

I slide my hand around Esperanza's hips to her buttocks, hook my thumb over the elastic, and pull downward. Esperanza raises her bottom, and as I help her shimmy out of her panties, I tell myself she isn't uncomfortable and her rigidity was only a pause between two movements. She seemingly corroborates my thoughts when she leaves the bed, reaches into her carryall, and returns with a condom she unrolls over my penis with her mouth.

As I watch Esperanza's head rise and fall, I regret my wife hasn't fellated me for at least nineteen years and only has intercourse with me once a week on Saturday or Sunday morning. It's my fault. I've tried my best to be a good husband by being loyal, protective, considerate, and giving. My wife was poor so I shared my wealth. She was uneducated so I paid for her college. Her clothes were Kmart and Walmart so we replaced them with Nordstrom and Saks Fifth Avenue. Despite the makeover, I've never discovered a scintilla of Julia in her. Although my wife is beautiful, she isn't as cute or smart or funny and she doesn't laugh or flirt or smell like her. Each day is a reminder of who she isn't. When she says, "You buy me jewelry, things, because you don't love me," I stifle the retort, "I can only discuss books with you if I read Danielle Steele."

Esperanza reclines, and as we have intercourse, stares wide-eyed into space and hums a song I don't recognize. Realizing she would rather be anywhere that isn't under a man like me, I wish I'd made her a drink. With each thrust, I feel more like a rapist than a john, having sex that's more neurotic than erotic, and so I contemplate sending her home.

Suddenly Esperanza grabs my hips and pulls me toward her, while she raises her pelvis to meet mine. She looks me in the eye and yells, "Harder!" She must have come to terms with our situation: she needs cash for food and shelter and other necessities and perhaps to buy some nonessential things, and I long to ejaculate in her. Those words become her mantra as she repeatedly bangs into me, giving me her version of a porn star experience, until I roll off her onto my back, panting and soaking with sweat.

While I listen to my heart pounding, I calculate that twenty years of marriage with sex once a week means I've had sex with my wife one thousand and forty times. Esperanza rests her head on my chest. "Thump, thump, thump," she says, while she taps me three times beneath my ribs. Then I realize the twentieth anniversary is eight weeks away so it's really one thousand and thirty-two times and that number doesn't take into account the many weekends my wife and I didn't have relations because we fought or the nightly sex we had before we married.

Esperanza's head slides to my stomach, and she fellates me again. After a while, as she raises her head, she puts her hand beneath her mouth and around my penis, pulls the condom off, and goes back down on me. It happens so quickly. One moment it's sheathed, I blink and it's bare, and her flesh is against mine. I'm horrified. My inattentiveness allowed a covered blow job to become bareback, and now it's too late, there's no way I can be un-sucked, and instead I'm stuck watching Esperanza's head move up and down while contemplating her swallowing other defenseless penises, which must have been serviced by other prostitutes, and all the other penises sucked and fucked by them, and the daisy chain of penises to prostitutes to penises to prostitutes that ex-tends from my room at the Marriott to the rest of Manhattan and the other boroughs of New York City, to Long Island and Upstate New York, to New Jersey and Connecticut, from one state to an-other, across the Atlantic and the Pacific, to Europe and Asia and around the globe, and the STDs lurking in them that now might have been transmitted to me.

I watch my penis disappear in Esperanza's mouth, then re-appear. The voice inside my head rattles off syphilis, gonorrhea, nongonococcal urethritis, granuloma inguinale, herpes, HPV, and HIV. It vanishes and reappears again. If Esperanza has been a prostitute for three weeks, assuming she worked seven days a week and was with one man a day, she has been with twenty-one men. If she took Sundays off, eighteen. Two men a day, with Sundays off, thirty-six. It passes out of sight, then it's back. If three a day, fifty-four. Four a day, seventy-two. If each man has been with even one other prostitute, who, like Esperanza, has worked for only three weeks, the numbers become too unwieldy to do in my head, particularly while Esperanza sucks my penis as if it were a Popsicle.

My worries vanish into the vortex of her mouth with my penis. What's done is done. I will go to a doctor when I'm home. He can test my urine and my blood, pull and prod my penis, lift and squeeze my testicles, and stick a finger in my anus. Then he can write me a prescription for an antibiotic, and I'll be good as new and my wife none the wiser.

I clench the sheets and tense my legs, ready to ejaculate. For a second I wish it could be in her vagina because that would be manlier. And then she lifts her head and doesn't go down again. She sticks her tongue out between pursed lips, pulls it back in, and grimaces as if she has tasted something terrible. I'm so disappointed her services don't include cum in mouth, I find little solace her stopping fellatio at the first sign of pre-ejaculatory fluid might minimize my risk of infection.

Esperanza places another condom on me and assumes the doggie position. As I move in and out of her, it's as if one phantom condom after another is rolled over the real one. Sensation decreases so I increase speed, but it doesn't help. When I approach the goal, it backs away. Attempting to reach it, I squat in the position my wife pejoratively calls "doing the monkey," and Esperanza gives me a wife experience by pushing me away.

I place Esperanza in the missionary position and thrust into her until I'm so exhausted I collapse beside her. She removes the condom and tosses it on the nightstand. She rests her head on my chest and says, "You were really good."

"I'm beat. I'm old." I'm feeling sorry for myself because I wasn't able to ejaculate. It's another failure to be added to what has become a long list: not being good at any sport; being rejected by my chosen college and law school; not marrying Julia and marrying a woman I didn't love; not having friends; not making partner and not being able to find a different position because I don't have clients; earning only five-eighths the compensation I should; and so many more. "I'm sixty."

"You don't seem it." Esperanza wraps her left arm around my shoulder. She strokes my stomach and kisses my chest, giving me a girlfriend experience. "I thought you were going to wear me out."

"Where are you from?" I ask.

"Brooklyn. You?"

"Connecticut."

"Why are you here?" Esperanza asks.

"A seminar."

"What do you do?"

"I'm a lawyer. What did you do before working for the escort service?"

"The same, except I," and Esperanza's voice breaks, "had a pimp." Her body quivers against mine as she murmurs between sobs. "I was his Saturday night mami, but the cops killed him."

"I'm sorry," I offer, thinking I should say or do something that will make her feel better. I do the only thing I can do; I enfold her in my arms.

Minutes later Esperanza is so still, anyone who saw us would mistake us for lovers. I should know better than anybody that appearances can deceive. By day I'm a lawyer, by night a john. I lie here in what looks like a lover's embrace, but I'm disgusted by her skin against mine now that I know she had a pimp who I imagine wore an ostentatious big hat and fur coat with a muffler made of multi-colored feathers, like Rooster on the TV series, *Baretta,* and she may have plied her trade for twenty or forty bucks a pop, or even multi-pops, in alleyways or backseats of cars. God only knows how many low-lifes she might have serviced before me. And yet I'm here. A low-life too. Me! It's unbelievable. I'm Jewish. I take my wife to Manhattan once a month to see a Broadway show.

Esperanza lightly snores. Wanting her to leave, I bounce to the edge of the mattress, but she doesn't stir. I hover over her, poised to shake her, while I wonder whether she's still here because she has nowhere to go. Maybe there's a homeless shelter, or worse, a box in an alleyway she doesn't want to return to. If she left, perhaps she would travel back and forth from Manhattan to Brooklyn on the subway until morning. But she should be able to afford a decent home. If the retail price is twice the wholesale price, she keeps one hundred of the two hundred dollars. Assuming she is with only one man each day, she earns thirty-six thousand five hundred dollars a year. Then I recall Esperanza's intermittent discomfort. Conceivably her experiences as a prostitute have made her ill, like soldiers who return home from war with PTSD. Maybe she's only capable of working sporadically. I have this theory: when people have sex without love, they're diminished; they lose a part of themselves. Each time I've had sex after Julia became my former girlfriend, even when the sex was with Julia, I experienced the feeling of nothingness. Perhaps both Esperanza and I are empty.

Instead of disturbing Esperanza's slumber, I lie awake beside her, concerned that if I fall asleep Esperanza will steal my wallet, watch, and iPhone, and given the circumstances, I won't be able to report the crime to the police. I take stock of my gifts to my wife of necklaces, bracelets, earrings, and rings in fourteen carat yellow and white gold, with natural diamonds, sapphires, rubies, emeralds, and tanzanite, and the pearls and the gold and other Swiss watches my wife has repeatedly introduced into evidence in the courtroom of our marriage to support her complaint that I don't love her. That jewelry must have cost me over one hundred thousand dollars, enough money to purchase, at the retail hourly rate of two hundred dollars, more than five hundred hours of Esperanza's time, and at the wholesale hourly rate of one hundred dollars, one thousand of the sexual encounters I've had with my wife.

When daylight breaks, the clock shows five eighteen. I shake Esperanza and say, "It's morning." She stirs, sits up, and jumps off the bed. She ponders me and the room. "You must have fallen asleep last night," I offer.

Esperanza rubs her eyes. "Oh, I'm sorry," she says. She picks up her panties, negligee, and satchel, and goes into the bathroom. After a while the sink runs, the toilet flushes, and she returns looking the same as when she first entered the room. She takes the money off the nightstand, kisses me on the cheek, whispers, "Thanks," and walks out the door.

Determined to finish what Esperanza and I started, I masturbate, but give up after about forty-five minutes. Then I shower to scrub Esperanza off me. As my lathered hands glide over my body, I have the urge to claw my skin, to rip it open beneath the surging water and watch the shame and guilt and self-hatred spill out and disappear down the drain. When I wash my gimcrack penis for the sixth time, this desire is replaced by the fleeting urge to yank it from its socket and flush it down the toilet.

After I dry off, I lie on the other bed to sleep the day away. I picture Esperanza retrieving the money from the nightstand. I remember her kiss on my cheek and feel badly I didn't give her a tip. I hear her crying. I recall she dressed and used the sink and toilet in the bathroom before she left, and she used the toilet and sink and undressed in the bathroom after she appeared. Her departure was a rewinding of her arrival; I wish it was an undoing that extended to the moment before I picked the *Village Voice* out of the bin.

Mostly Harmless:
The Gospel According to Tim

Trevor D. Richardson

Luke thought about his dead grandmother when he masturbated.

Not like that though. Not like he thought about her, thought about her. That'd be weird. I realize now that I might have put words like "necrophilia" and "incest" into your heads and that was definitely not my intention. Bad narrating on my part, my bad. I'm really not much good at telling stories, but I wanted to tell this one. What I meant to say is, Luke thought about her looking down on him from Heaven and just being disappointed. You know, like her face all sad up there and stuff.

He could see her up there in a white dress, sitting on a cloud, knitting – she was always knitting, so he figured she'd be one of those knitting angels instead of the ones that play harps or whatever. Then she would look down and see him just pounding on his little adolescent flesh saber like a frustrated ape and start crying or something. I don't know, I can't remember all the details. I'm telling you what Luke told me, it really should be him telling it, but it's embarrassing so he won't. I'm telling it because, to me, it seems like that's what Heaven does to you, you know? It's like, without a Heaven you're just a kid trying to get some hormonal rage out because you're twelve and sex right now is a terrible, awful, maybe should be illegal kind of idea. But you can't just walk around with a rage boner, you against the world either. Without Heaven, Luke looking at that magazine ad of the naked girl all crouched behind her smooth legs so you can't really see anything but you feel like you do would be fine. Sort of like, without sex, that picture would just be a girl showing you that her hair removal cream works really well. It's all about context and influence. Sex changes your thinking – so does Heaven.

Luke grew up guilty. We all did, all of us that believed in God, anyway. But his was the worst. That's not really what I want to talk about though. There isn't anything I can say about believing in God, or how screwed up it made all of us, that you haven't really heard already. I do want to say that I think the stuff with priests touching kids and stuff, while terrible, has taken the focus off of a larger issue. You don't have to get molested by the clergy to get all screwed up by them. It's like Luke worrying that his dead grandma could see him wanking it. You get this unhealthy relationship to your world and it messes with everything.

There was this one night when we were both twenty-two – Christ, twenty-two, it feels like a zillion years ago or something. We were hanging out at Luke's apartment and his wife was out of town, so it was just the two of us. It felt like high school again. Not just because we were hanging out, one-on-one, like the old days, but even the little things like how Luke would worry what would happen if he drank or smoked or said bad words. Like I brought over some Jameson and smoke and he was like, "Okay, but we can't let Denise find out."

Then I'm all, "You haven't changed a bit, man. If it isn't, 'I don't think God wants us to be drinking' then it's 'We can't let Denise find out.'"

Luke says, "You trying to say Denise is my new Jesus?"

"Hey, you said it, not me, pal. But don't worry, I won't go into the whole 'Thou shalt have no other gods before me' thing if you just pour a couple and pipe down – you'll feel loads better, I promise."

Things were just like that. We gave each other a hard time, like guys do, you know? Sure you know, you've seen TV. So we have our little tumblers full of scotch whiskey and we like clink them together all douchey-like and we sip in silence.

A minute or so goes by and Luke finally goes, "Okay, so not exactly like high school, right? By now we'd be blasting some band that we'd cringe at now and we'd probably be jumping on the furniture."

"Or playing Goldeneye on your shitty 64."

He laughs, sips the scotch, and goes, "Or playing Goldeneye while bouncing on the furniture."

We fell silent again after that and I go, "Dude. What's with you?"

"What do you mean?" he asks.

"I mean 'what's with you?' It's like you're not even here or something," I get this wave and say, "How's married life treating you? You've been together, what? A year now or something?"

"Sixteen months."

I remember thinking how weird it was that he said sixteen months. Honestly, a lot of this is just me trying to paraphrase how it all went down as best as I remember it. It's sort of like trying to retell a dream, you know what happened, but no matter how much you talk it doesn't feel quite right. It's like you are always leaving something out, but you don't know what. Anyway, I do remember that "sixteen months" thing, that part was an exact quote. I remember it depressed the hell out of me because it sounded like the way parents track their toddler's age in months, you know? Timmy's fourteen months old. That kind of thing. It seemed really shitty, measuring the age of your marriage like the age of that screaming, crapping thing that keeps you up nights. God, it really brought me down.

I go, "Fuck me."

And Luke shouts, "Whoa, language, bro!"

He even looked around, like Denise was going to appear from behind the sofa and yell at him for letting someone bring that kind of profanity into her home.

I downed the last of my scotch in one swallow and, pouring myself another, said, "She ain't here, man, no one's here. I don't know what you're so worried about."

"What? I'm not worried. Who's worried?" Luke says.

"You're looking around like you're worried your wife is watching you on Nanny Cam. Hell, she might be for all I know, but that doesn't change anything. If a man wants to say 'fuck,' he should just say 'fuck.'"

"Denise and I try to hold ourselves to a higher standard is all."

I fire back, "You mean, Denise holds you to her standards and you go along with it."

"You got a problem with my wife, dude?"

I sigh and set down my drink. Leaning back into the sofa, I say, "No, it's not that exactly. But I know she has a problem with me. I seem to recall a time where she called me a low-life and 'the worst type of sinner.' The 'backslidden' Christian, as she called it, is worse than the ignorant non-believer."

Luke froze. He wouldn't look at me or nothing. He just sat there, staring at this framed picture on the wall of some Rennaisance painting of Jesus and Mary, like after he's off the cross or whatever and she's holding his body and crying. Hell of a thing to have in your living room, come to think of it.

Finally, Luke goes, "How do you know about that?"

I tell him the story. It was the night of the rehearsal dinner for his wedding. I had gotten kind of drunk and fell over onto this little table thing. It wasn't a particularly important table, as far as tables go, even as far as tables in weddings go – because, let's face it, there are a lot of random tables involved in a wedding set up. This one was just meant to hold the guest book thing, and the guest book wasn't even on it yet since it was the rehearsal and all. Anyway, I got drunk and I fell over, not like passed out, I was just goofing and I slipped. It doesn't matter. The point is, they were in the car fighting about it and it was, like, this really big deal to her.

Turns out Luke's phone had pocket-dialed and I got a whole, uncut, nine-minute segment of the fight in which she said, "I don't know why you hang out with that guy, he's a loser, a total low-life."

Luke says, "He's my oldest friend."

And Denise says, "That doesn't matter. Sometimes finding righteousness means letting go of the past and moving forward. You should be thinking about the future, thinking about me."

"I don't see why I should have to choose," Luke says, sounding really wussy or whatever.

Denise says, "This isn't a 'it's him or me' argument, Luke. I'm concerned for you, for your future, for your spirit. You are poisoning your heart by keeping someone like Timothy around. He's the worst type of sinner, this is someone that has seen the face of God and chosen to ignore it. He has grieved the Holy Spirit by rejecting Him. He has actively chosen his sin. The difference between an ignorant non-believer and a backslidden Christian, like Tim, is that he saw the right path and went against it, deciding he would rather indulge in sin. And this is the man you call your best friend?"

Things kind of devolved from there, I won't go into it. But those were the particulars. Anyway, I laid it all out for Luke and he just sits there again. I can imagine him doing this same thing when fighting with Denise. Or, I guess, letting Denise yell at him. That's probably more accurate. Him just sitting there, staring at Dead Jesus in his underwear and his crying mom while his wife just preaches at him.

Since he wasn't saying anything, I just go, "Look, dude, I came here to have a good time with you for a change. It's been ages since we just hung out. I don't want to argue with you, what do you say we just drop it and hook up a game or something?"

Luke smiles and nods, "I'd like that," he says, "You want another drink?"

"You even gotta ask?"

He pours two more and finishes off the Jameson bottle. After that he went for this little side closet thing with this dusty, crappy looking little plastic tub. He pulls it out and I know it's where he keeps all his video game stuff. Like, I just know it instantly, I can see the whole story plastered all over the side of that dusty bin. His wife says she doesn't want it out where people can see it, like it's one thing to still play games like a child, it's another to have them visible in a modern, mature home. So he hides them away and hasn't played anything in months by the look of it.

We hook up his Nintendo 64 and start playing Goldeneye 007 for old time's sake. For us, it didn't matter how far video games advanced, that was still the most fun two guys could have together playing a multiplayer game. Best first person shooter ever.

My Jameson runs out and Luke hits pause, running into the kitchen to find something. I remember that real well. Like, he was all proper, a gracious host, and I felt like his wife had him so trained that he didn't even realize he was doing it.

I said, "Man, you don't have to serve me. I'm your best friend, not a house guest for a business dinner."

"I know, I know...it's just habit. Listen, we don't have much, but I do have this bottle of old whiskey from a party last year."

He explains where it comes from so I don't think he bought it for himself.

"Is it in a plastic bottle?" I asked.

He goes, "Yeah, how'd you know?"

"Because I brought it over here last year. My ex-girlfriend bought it to put in her Coke and then left it when we split. I thought I could get you guys to drink it since you don't know shit about whiskey and wouldn't know how terrible it is."

Luke, from the kitchen, yells, "Dude, it's in a plastic bottle! You don't have to be Hunter Thompson to know it's shit whiskey."

That was the first time I really laughed all evening and it was a really good laugh.

Not much happened for a while. We got really drunk on that shit whiskey, what we started calling the shit-skey. Then I brought out the smoke and, after a very half-hearted debate, Luke joined in. There's sort of a gap in my memory here, but I do remember the main part, the whole reason I wanted to tell you this weird story.

It's late in the evening and we are properly trashed.

Luke goes, "Dude, I'm totally blitzed."

"Luke," I say, "no one says 'blitzed' anymore."

"Naw, man, you don't get it. I'm blitzed, like in the literal sense, like all these chemicals are little German bombers flying over my brain and dropping bombs in a sustained, aerial attack. Just wearing me down...it's the Blitzkrieg up there, man."

I laughed pretty hard at that one too, one of those kinds of laughs where you're like, "Oh, yeah, this is why this dude is my best friend. Almost forgot..."

At this point, the menu screen for Goldeneye was the only light source in the room, hovering there after a battle with our stats and ranking. On Luke's side of the screen it says, "Mostly Harmless," a little inside joke from the game developers that also happened to be Douglas Adams fans, I guess. On my side, "Most Cowardly." Not exactly a match for the ages. "Most Cowardly" typically meant you spent a lot of time shooting people in the back or when they were unarmed.

Christ, I'm a piece of shit. Leave it to videogames to show you your true self.

We sat there in that haze of green light, the orange ember of my glass pipe flaring up and dying out as we passed the smoke. Very little was said on account of us being so "blitzed."

Then, like out of nowhere, Luke says, "You remember that winter church camp, man? The one where you got so mad?"

"Yeah, man, I don't tend to forget about things that get me that mad."

He smiles in the haze and says, "Yeah, you really wigged out, man. What was it you punched again? I remember it was plaster, was it that big fake cross?"

Laughing, I say, "Hell, I wish...probably would've if it was closer to me. No, it was that stone pillar thing, you know the one that they had all that fake ivy on and shit? They used it in that pageant one of those years to tell the story of Samson. I put my fist through that about six times, blood and skin all over it."

"You broke your hand. Had to go to the hospital. I remember that part."

"Yeah," I say, "what brought that up, dude? Feeling like punching through something?"

He says, "No, I was just thinking about what got you so mad. That year the winter camp was an all boys thing, remember? They split it up because people were just going to church camp and getting a girlfriend for a week. We had that counselor dude, Corey or Cody, something..."

"Cobie."

"Christ, his name was actually Cobie? Fuck me."

I laughed, this was the Luke I remembered from, like, when we were kids, before Denise and church and all that stuff. Anyway, yeah, get a few drinks in him and you get to see the rebellious eighth grade kid again.

He says, "Cobie sat us down and did that whole speech."

I told you I'm not much of a narrator so I'm gonna stop writing this whole thing in dialogue format. The whole back and forth is too hard to maintain. He said. I said. I said. He said. I said quietly... he said emphatically. It's hard to write. Can't be much fun to read. Let me just tell you what happened.

We were at this church camp over Christmas break, sophomore year, I think. It was kind of out in the sticks, but Luke and

I knew it real well because we would sometimes go out there and volunteer in the summer. You know, move stuff or dig ditches or whatever they needed. It made us feel like we were doing more for God than giving him ten percent, you know, like that. The people that ran the place were sort of strange – Arlo and Mary. Like, you could always see how frayed and tired Arlo and Mary were, their marriage was sort of visibly stretched, their eyes sort of gray. That kind of thing. Whenever we asked how they were doing, they would always go into their laundry list of problems, like, "Oh... the well pump is out again and we're down three staff members this month and the bills are piling up and..."

You get the idea.

Anyway, the point is, they would always end it with the same phrase and it really got under my skin. After their list of complaints, they would go, "Yay, God!"

It was meant to be kind of a refrain to keep them centered or whatever, like George Costanza's dad going, "Serenity Now!" Only it came off real sarcastic-like, you know? Yay, God! What the hell is that?

So we're at the church camp and there's snow everywhere. One day they sit all the boys down in a little huddle and this Cobie fucker goes, "All right, guys, it's time we had a serious discussion."

Right away, I know what this means. It all sort of clicked, right? They separated the boys from the girls and here we are having a serious discussion. I could see the committee meeting, some old fucker saying it's real important that we sit these boys down and give 'em a talkin' to about tuggin' the tadpole. Like, fuck Jesus, we need to discuss masturbation habits with a bunch of teenagers.

This masturbation thing is an epidemic!

I want you to imagine that last part in the voice of Patton Oswalt screaming.

So I looked over at Luke and he was doing that thing where he looks down or away if he's ashamed. Remember how this all started? Luke always thought of his dead grandmother when he masturbated. He was thinking of her right now. More than God, more than Christ, more than the devil, Luke always had some woman in his life that he felt was frowning down on him. His mother, his dead grandma, Denise...Mother Mary, whoever.

Cobie says, "We need to talk about that thing we all struggle with, but no one ever talks about."

Now, right away I'm irritated. Admittedly, I was also a little impressed, because it takes some serious balls to sit down a bunch of freshmen and sophomores in high school and talk to them about masturbation. Still, it was the way it was done that bothered me. I don't care about talking about jacking off, it's part of life, who cares? I wasn't like Luke. I never thought of it as anything but my own business. I didn't see how or why God should have an opinion about it. I didn't care what anyone thought, this was me making me feel good.

Like that line in *Annie Hall*, "Don't knock masturbation, it's sex with someone I love."

I liked doing it and didn't accept that it was a sin. I just wouldn't. I mean, if you put it all out in a line, there's these church people saying, "Don't have sex before marriage, don't think about women, don't lust, don't masturbate..." The rules on sex seemed like they could just come down to one idea, "Sex is for making babies only. Never, ever enjoy it."

Luke was all in that philosophy. He had that Christian shame about sex that has kept him repressed and fucked up for his whole life. He couldn't talk about it, couldn't admit it. He would go as long as he possibly could without doing it and then he would "succumb." He would talk to me about it sometimes and it always sounded like an alcoholic telling you how he fell off the wagon.

"Man, Tim, I made it almost three weeks this time, but now I'm back at zero."

Then he would quote the Bible, usually something from the Apostle Paul about the flesh being weak or whatever. It was sickening.

So Cobie, the dorky camp counsilor with the cystic acne and the blonde facial hair that's barely there, says, "Your body is a temple of the Holy Spirit. It is our responsibility, as children of God, to keep that temple pure for the Lord. When you abuse your body in this way, you aren't just making yourself impure, you're making your temple impure. When you think about those women or you look at those pictures or videos on the internet, you are degrading yourself, the people you're thinking about, and even your heavenly father. I just..."

"Excuse me," I said, raising my hand.

Cobie's eyes lit up with hope, an expression that seemed to exclaim how he thought he was getting through to us, "Yes, Tim," he said, "you have a question?"

"Yeah, I do," I replied, "I thought the Holy Spirit was supposed to purify us, not the other way around."

"Beg pardon?"

"I thought that when we accept Christ as our savior and let the Holy Spirit enter our hearts, that it was meant to purify us of sin so that we can go to Heaven."

"Yes," Cobie says, "Yes, that's true."

"But you're saying that we can make the temple of the spirit impure by cumming."

Cobie blushed and some of the other kids snickered. If you hadn't already guessed, this was kind of the tail end of my time as a believer in Christ. I had a lot of questions, and no one seemed to know how to answer them.

"Okay, okay," Cobie said, "let's keep it mature, boys. We need to be comfortable with these ideas if we are going to have this discussion. But, Tim, let's try to keep it classy, shall we?"

"Well, what should I call it that sounds classy then? There's nothing classy about shooting your load."

"True," Cobie said, chuckling and blushing at the same time, "Don't say 'shooting your load,' say 'ejaculating.' The Bible calls it 'spreading your seed.' You could say that if you want."

"Thanks, I'm good," I reply, "But you didn't answer my question, Mr. Cobie."

Cobie tried to say that having the Holy Spirit should make us want to live a pure life, that it isn't about us dirtying the Holy Spirit, but dirtying ourselves. To which I tried to say he ought to be able to clean us up again, it's sort of his job. Cobie then went on to say that faith in Christ isn't a free pass to sin and I asked him to show me where in the Bible it says masturbating was a sin. Cobie said it was "sexual immorality" and the Bible has lots to say about sexual immorality.

I asked him to show me where it says, "Thou shalt not pull your pud until you splooge daddy porridge" and that was when he yelled at me and said I was being inappropriate.

Then the argument kind of escalated. He said I was backsliding into hell. I told him he was giving kids an unhealthy complex about a safe and natural way to handle urges. He said it was the Christian's job to overcome temptation, not give in to it. After that, I quoted Oscar Wilde, "I can resist anything, except temptation."

That one kind of cracked me up. It's not often you get to mix in some Oscar Wilde with a religious debate about God's stance on male pleasure.

Then Luke stepped in. He said, "Tim, Cobie is right. Haven't you ever felt it? That shame after you're done?"

To which I replied, "No. No, I haven't."

Cobie twisted the knife, "The only way you can feel that shame, that conviction of the spirit, is if you have the Holy Spirit inside you. Are you sure you're saved, Tim?"

That's when it all kind of hit me at once. I thought about this time where Luke said he thought about killing himself because he couldn't stop masturbating and he was so tired of the guilt. He said he couldn't live like that anymore. He said he didn't even look at porn or anything, but he still couldn't resist. I thought about all the arguments, all the alienation at school – on both sides – the stuff we were taught to say to people, and the stuff they said to us. I thought about how we had been trained to view our own bodies, even our own minds, as the enemy, and I suddenly felt like I was being conditioned, you know? Like, you hear about those old MK Ultra programs where they pump guys full of psychedelics to break down their identities and rebuild them as killers. It felt just like that, I don't know how else to explain it. I felt sick, I felt mad, and I felt so angry that they had done all this to my friend. He was right in there with them, telling me I was bad, telling me that touching myself was going to send me to Hell and if I didn't feel bad about it then I was practically there already. And then I snapped out of it and my knuckles were bloody and I had broken this pillar that someone tied a fake Samson to the year prior.

I let out a sigh. On the screen, the awards kept flashing: Mostly Harmless, Most Cowardly.

Luke goes, "Yeah, I'm sorry about that, man. I was so in the wrong on that one. After they sent you home, how long was it?"

"What? You mean, after they made me do the walk of shame to that white van like a school shooter, how long was it that we didn't speak?"

"Um...yeah, that's what I mean. I guess..."

"Seventeen days."

"We didn't talk for seventeen days? You remember the exact number?"

I go, "Yeah. It was three days after we had been back in school and you said our chemistry teacher, what's his name?"

"Mr. Glover."

"Yeah, you said Mr. Glover's head looked like a cock and balls. Then we laughed and got kicked out of class. That was how we made up. I think you decided that I was just a heathen after that, because you never talked about Jesus or the Christian shame again. But we were still friends."

Luke sighed and took a long drag off the bowl. He said, "Man, I'm sorry, man. I thought I was so high and mighty. You know I thought I was better than you?"

"Yeah, I know. Kinda thought you still did."

"No, not anymore. Not me."

"What's going on with you, Luke? Why did you ask me over?"

There was a really, really long quiet after that. I heard the air rushing through the pipe as he pulled on it again, but there wasn't really anything left to smoke. He was kind of just pulling on ash and air and not really much else. I took it from him and started repacking it.

Finally, Luke goes, "You know how we would talk about porn in our prayer meetings, back when you still used to go? It was like this big struggle for all the guys, you know?"

"Except you, I remember that. You said you hadn't succumbed. That was your word, 'succumbed.' You were still an internet porn virgin or whatever."

"Yeah, I still succumbed in other ways, but I never got into the internet porn so much. You don't know this, dude, but that was one of the reasons why Denise wanted to marry me. Can you believe that? I told her I'd never gotten into internet porn, which was true, and she was so relieved and impressed that her weird little conservative lady brain went, 'Bing! This is a good one!'"

I laughed pretty hard at that, but didn't say anything.

Luke continued, "She was nuts about it, man. I swear to God, it's like the only thing I think she's thinking about sometimes. Like, how to not let me think about other women. If there's a set of tits on a movie, she instantly shoots me this look and I have to turn my head away like when we were kids and watched *Titanic* with your mom. Remember that? She made us cover our eyes during that art scene, but we looked anyway. Anyway, yeah, so it's like that all the time. It's even out in public, you know? Like, if there's a hot chick, she gets all bent out of shape, even if I don't even see her or look at her, she's just upset because someone pretty exists."

"Sounds like she's got some insecurity that has nothing to do with you, man."

"I know!" Luke shouts, "But that's not the worst part, man, um... ugh," he sort of starts to slur and stumble, maybe like he's losing his nerve or about to puke, or both. I can tell it's something important he needs to say, so I just wait. Finally, he says, "So we waited till we got married, you know? Like you're supposed to or whatever. We were virgins when we got married."

"I know," I said, cutting him off a little at the end there, "it's one of the things I always respected about you guys. I mean, I couldn't have done it, but I think it's cool that you did."

Luke sighs again, this time blowing blue smoke across the television screen, "Yeah, except it was one of those things, those like Christian cool things, you know? Like, it was cool to other Christians because we did it, we proved we could do it and we won. That was the whole thing with us, we wanted to win at being Christian. I got that music pastor job, we got married young, we saved ourselves, it was the whole dream, you know? Everything you're supposed to do, according to the church or Jesus or God, we did it."

"Yeah, so? I thought that's what you wanted or believed in or whatever."

"It is... it was. I don't know, I'm all fucked up. What I'm trying to say is, I'm watching porn now and Denise knows it."

"Whoa, what?" I say, kind of blurting it out like a real idiot. I do that sometimes, blurt out.

He goes, "Yeah, I know, right?"

"Jesus," I say, "After all that. What the hell happened, man? I mean, I know for me it was really hard to stop masturbating after I started having sex. Like, I knew how good I could feel and it made me know how good I didn't feel, so I'd get on the computer. Sometimes even in, like, the same day that I already had sex with my girlfriend or something, you know?"

"Yeah, I get it now," Luke replied, "but it's worse than that. I just have to tell somebody, I think that's why I had you come over. I need to say this to someone or I might just walk into traffic or something."

"Go ahead, bro, you know there's nothing you can say that I'll judge you for. I've done way worse."

Luke started to cry right then. I remember, it was like he was crying for what he'd done or what he wanted to tell me, but the thing that broke him was when I said that thing about me not judging. After a lot of snot and sobs and stuff, he said, "I never realized the kind of simple love you can get from people that don't believe in God. You know, man?"

"No, I guess I don't."

Keep in mind, he was like sobbing and coughing and this was all really unintelligible. I'm sort of translating for you, more because I don't know how to write spit sounds and stutters because I'm not a very good writer. So, just, for my sake or whatever, keep in mind that this is all just like the grossest, vomity, trashy, man weeping you ever heard and somewhere in all of that he says, "I mean, with Christians they have this way of ranking you as a good or bad Christian. The pastors talk about the Ten Commandments and the priests know what every sin is worth and how many Hail Marys you gotta say or whatever. Then I talk to you and you're just like, 'Cool, bro, I'm fucked up too.' I feel like I don't want to believe in God anymore because all it ever did is make me feel worthless like I wanna die."

All I could tell him was that was why I bailed on it and then he says, "I didn't know what Denise's body looked like when we got married."

He sort of makes this sucking sound right here, sort of like he was pulling all his snot and tears back up into his face to compose himself, you know? He does that sound and then says, "We were good and all, like I said. But nothing prepared me for how I would feel when we finally did it. It was our wedding night and, well..."

"Just say it, man, were you bad at it and so you started watching porn to learn how it works?"

"No, nothing like that. I was actually all right. It was Denise."

"Denise was bad?"

"Well, yeah, she was all over the place, but that's not the worst part."

I ask him what the worst part was.

Luke said, "Her boobs were ugly. No one ever told me boobs could be ugly. I had no idea. It was, like, weird nipple to boob-flesh ratio, you know? And she had these folds above, kind of coming from her armpit. Like, you ever seen when ladies wear those strapless gowns to awards shows and stuff?"

"Yeah, I've seen awards shows, Luke."

"Ever notice how, like, the ones with really big boobs get that sort of crease on top, kinda going from their armpits over the top of their cleavage. It's not real nice to look at, but you kind of don't think much of it because it's just their boobs getting all pressed and compacted and folded up in the dress, right?"

"I mean, yeah... I guess so."

Luke goes, "That's just how Denise looks all the time. I can have her flat on her back and there's these creases there. I don't like it."

"How does that translate to pornography, pal? You're losing me."

Luke kind of wipes his face and stuff and says, "Oh, yeah, so um... I started looking for pictures of girls with breasts that look like hers. When I could find some it made me feel a little better."

I sort of pick up my empty drink glass and swirl it around, trying to find some residue to drink on or whatever. I guess I wanted my hands busy or something. Anyway, while I'm doing that I say, "Do you think you were trying to train your cock to get up for girls that look like Denise? I mean, I've done it before. I always liked girls with bigger chests, but then I dated this girl that was, like, pretty flat, you know? I watched a bit of what they call 'petite' girl porn and got to where I liked it. You know, it actually helped. Next thing you know, she was like the most beautiful, sexy thing in the world to me, right? Was it something like that?"

"Maybe, kinda... I don't know. I think mainly I just wanted to know she wasn't the only one or something. Maybe I was trying to retrain my pecker, maybe...but you might be givin' me too much credit. Whatever the case, it's not working. I'm miserable. And Denise knows it, man. She found out because I'm an amateur and don't know dick about clearing browser history."

"Yeah, I was just gonna say, 'Sure hope you're clearing your browser history.'"

Luke forces an awkward laugh and says, "Well, no, she found it and we had this huge fight, but not the yelling kind with passion and stuff. Like, a quiet, calm, rational fight like when your mom lectures you or whatever. Then she just cried for like four hours and said I betrayed her. She called me a liar, you know? She said I told her I didn't do that and I should know how much it bothers her. She said she felt like I cheated on her because Jesus says what you do in your mind or your heart is the same as doing it for real."

I interrupt, "Dude, first of all... no. That's not true at all. If it were, we'd all be up on murder charges every time we drove a car. This is the kind of shit that made me quit the church. They say that in resisting temptation, in facing that challenge and rising above it, you are honoring God, but then they turn around and say that if you have a bad thought, which is the same as being tempted, that you have already committed the sin in your heart. Fuck that. You can't have it both ways. She's totally off base, man,

I mean, sure, if she doesn't like porn that's her prerogative as your wife or whatever, but she doesn't get to say what you did is as bad as cheating on her. That's bogus."

"Anyway, she gave me an ultimatum. She said if it happens again she'll divorce me for being unfaithful. She even took the wireless router with her to work the other day because I was going to be home alone."

My brain screamed, "SHE DID WHAT?!" But I didn't say anything, I kept my cool. You'd be proud of me, I swear to God, you would. I did a good job.

I tried to console him as best I could, but I saw his plight. I mean, he couldn't say he got into it after they got married because that would lead to more questions. Luke said he didn't want to break her heart, you know? He loves her, she's his wife, and he didn't want to make her sad when she already has obvious issues with self-esteem and stuff.

I said, "So you would rather let this woman you made this solemn vow to, in front of God and everybody, think that you are a liar and a pervert than tell her the truth?"

"Yeah, I would rather let her think less of me than make her feel bad about herself. It would crush her, man. I mean, she's cried because I glanced at a girl's thong when she bent over in the supermarket, what's she gonna do if she finds out her ugly tits gave me a porn addiction?"

"Fuck, man, you're right. This is some serious shit."

"I know. I'm not asking you to figure it out for me, Tim. I just had to say it out loud and I knew I could trust you. You want some wine? I think I have a little bit of a box of wine left in the fridge."

I tell him sure and avoid the ridicule about having a box of wine, too obvious – too easy.

We didn't talk much about it after that. We drank and played some more 64 and tried to laugh. I remember how, at one point, he asked me why so many men struggle with porno. I remember he said "porno" and thought it was funny 'cause most guys say "porn" now. All I could think to tell him was how so many men struggle with their urges not synching up with their lady's. You know what I mean? It's like, you want to do it, but they don't. Both feelings are valid in the relationship, but it's her pussy and what she says goes. So you just feel deflated, you feel like your desires don't matter, you even get mad. I said to Luke, it's like things are always on their schedule because we're going into them, you know? I think porn is so enticing because it's this fantasy world where all the women are just up for it, like all that baggage and complication is just gone, just non-existent. All it takes to get laid is just a couple of cheesy lines and proximity. That's the man's fantasy, I think, like you wish you could get married to someone that you think is hot and perfect and cool and you want to spend your life with them, and you tell yourself it will be easier to have sex because you've done all the hard work of getting together and now they're just there with you, all the time, forever. Only that's not true because they're a person with their own stuff going on and nothing is what you thought. That's what I think anyway, but I'm not married, so what do I know?

I haven't seen Luke since that night. We passed out in the living room, really drunk and fucked up, and Denise said she had to come home early from her conference. Something about bad weather or something, I don't know. She found us in a heap of empty bottles and dirty glasses and weed ash and stink. The game screen was still on, flashing: Shortest Innings, Mostly Harmless. Over and over.

She yelled and screamed and I got mad and wound up saying how she had ugly tits and needed to lighten up. That was when they both threw me out, Luke too, which is understandable now, looking back. Last I heard they were getting a divorce. Denise started cheating on him when she found out about the porn. I thought that was kind of weird, it was like she felt justified or something, like Luke started it and she was gonna finish it. Like, in her eyes, Jesus gave her permission or something. I don't know. I remember wondering if the conference was even real or if she was with some guy.

I went home that night and looked for girls with ugly boobs on the internet for three hours and felt bad for my friend. I'm still waiting for him to show up at my apartment with a box of stuff and that bin of video games. I'll ask him about the divorce and he'll say, "Mostly Harmless."

The Curve of Spee

Mike Sauve

"Another succubus attack," I said to Charles, "Kayla St. Clair this time."

Charles and I wrote about 300 or 400 words of copy a day at Precision Marketing, and were usually finished before 10 am. The rest of the day we spent on 4chan's paranormal board /x/, which gave us the same frame of reference concerning succubus attacks.

"Me too," Charles said, "Almost worth the total pillaging of my energy. Some kind of space cocoon."

"Space cocoon, yes, mind-meld in a space cocoon. Wow. Are you still practicing magic?" I asked.

"I've gotten away from capital-M magic per se, but I am working with energy."

"Well, you better quit whatever you're doing. This dreaming the same dream business is where I'd like to get off this particular ride."

I quickly wrote a few paragraphs describing a new brand of vaginal cubes, and then went to Amy Bowman's Facebook profile. Her cover photo revealed her and Kayla St. Clair lounging in beach chairs at her parents' cabin outside town. Amy looked similar to when I'd last seen her towards the end of high school, except the light of youth had been extinguished.

"Charles. Our dream was not just shared, but prophetic bro! What kind of energy work are you doing?" I asked.

"Just the standard stuff. Projecting into the psychic ether, some rudimentary remote viewing," Charles said.

I queried Cleverbot.com on the matter. Some on /x/ believed the Cleverbot software to be a sort of modern oracle. As usual, its response was non-oracular, albeit syntactically-sound, nonsense.

Charles said, "I'm going to fap in the handicap washroom," and left with his laptop.

"See you in a bit," I said.

When Charles came back I borrowed his laptop and also went to fap. I checked his browser history expecting to see screen grabs from the *Experiencing Evelyn* episode where a teen-age Kayla St. Clair played in the big beach volleyball tournament. Goodness knows we'd both fapped to those screen grabs a time or two. But his history revealed he'd fapped to 3D Monster Porn. Due to too-frequent fapping we both needed weirder and weirder content to fap to, so I also quickly fapped to the 3D monsters using their macro-cocks to inflict internal damage on tiny maidens.

When I got back Charles had a plan. "This is the e-book man," he said.

Charles had released two occult-themed e-books. I had released one e-book, a picaresque. While neither of us had done well, we frequently discussed collaboration.

Our boss rarely came to our floor, so we emailed our work a little earlier than usual and took off in Charles' dads' Corolla.

I remembered Amy's camp from the odd party or afternoon spent there in high school. I'd been in love with her, as I'd been with all my female friends, but she hadn't loved me back, perhaps due to acne, or the somewhat stupid sound of my voice. We hadn't talked in years.

We pulled into Amy's drive. No lights on in the cabin. I noticed embers of a recently-extinguished fire.

"Anybody here?" I yelled.

"Mark?" Amy responded from a floating dock 20 metres off-shore. "Swim out to us. Guess who's out here with me?"

"Kayla St. Clair," I said.

"How'd you know?"

"Facebook."

"And a prophetic dream!" shouted Charles. I shot him a look = 'Shut up about the prophetic dream. I haven't seen this girl in years and used to love her, plus Kayla St. Clair doesn't need to be hearing about our prophetic dreams, this isn't /x/.'

We removed our duds, leaving our underwear on for propriety sake, and swam out to the dock. Amy kissed me on the lips. Something she'd always refused to do. Even in a game of spin the bottle once = 'We are too good of friends for that and it would be weird' but really = 'It will mean too much for Mark and be weird.'

Upon reaching the dock I had that sinking feeling like when you almost fall asleep but then don't. We all levitated in some kind of five-feet-above-the-floating-dock sky womb. Forgive me for straining narrative credulity here, but that's what happened. I can't describe it any other way: floating above dock, sky womb, maybe sky bubble if you prefer. Some of you may wish to stop reading now.

In the sky womb the collective memories of Amy, K. St. St. Clair, Charles and me were merged so that access to all the memories flooded our now-fused consciousness. It was painful to observe Amy's dismissive memories relative to me. Also in the mix were my memories of pining for her. Thank goodness for the ego dissolution occurring. In that sky-womb I was as much Amy as I was Mark; as Kayla as Charles.

With too much content to divulge without years of effort, I'll act as curator and narrate two thematically linked scenes: one traditional memory of Charles', and one future memory of Kayla St. Clair. Charles' is told in standard omniscient perspective.

With Kayla's, the tenses get a bit wonky because you try writing a memory from the future Jack.

Kayla

Kayla St. Clair was, still is, but won't always be, a Canadian television actress best-known for the most successful sitcom in Canadian television history; in other words, a sitcom seen by about twelve people who didn't work on it or fap to the screen grabs. Cocooned, enbubbled if you prefer, we remembered her youth acting camps, we remembered her first break on a Sears commercial, and I could relate all sorts of picayune anecdotes about ACTRA and Telefilm, but mercifully will not. Having viewed the future, having seen where it's taking the likes of Charles, myself, and our 4chan /b/rothers, I need to serve as the oracle Cleverbot can't quite manage to.

The year is 2027. Same worldline. This is not some alternate dimension gimmick. This is *our* future. Her fame behind her, no one watching Canadian TV or any kind of TV anymore, Kayla is handing out resumes at the mall, but those lucky enough to have jobs give looks = 'Yeah, right,' due to recent economic downturns. She sits (or *she will sit,* you see how this gets tricky) in food court desolation.

"Can I have those fries?" she asks a man clearing his tray. She doesn't feel shame about such a scummy fry request because she says it in a way she considers playful, plus doesn't have $41.50 for fries thanks.

"Why sure, my darling," the man says, creeping Kayla out, handing her his fry bag. "May I sit down?"

"Think I'm good with just the fries," Kayla will say.

"My name is Don Steel."

"Pleasure Don," Kayla says, "You don't know anyone who's hiring around here do you?"

"Depends on the work you're looking for."

The tone of Don's voice makes her want to leave the food court. But the fries tether her to both man and table, at least until she can finish the fries, so she sticks six fries in her mouth.

"Clerical, retail, whatever. I'm an actress but you know," she'll say, not sure if he knows or not, Canadian television being so infrequently viewed even in its heyday, and television as a medium such a distant artifact by then.

"Hmm," says future Don Steel, "Hmm now. I myself am a producer of films. Experiential films of the mind my dear."

"Neuropornography," says Kayla.

"Why now, I prefer the term Erotic Art. My operation is first-rate. Clean, private."

She rises to leave.

"$5,000 for an hour. Nobody touches you. I won't even be in the same room."

Minutes after the invention of Verisimilitudinous In-Brain Content, all normal narrative VIB content will be pushed to the farthest corners of niche demand as the demand for pornographic VIBs soars spike-like, soaring past demand for all other consumer products by exponential levels, downright devastating every other commodity market, from steel (who needs a car) to corn (money spent on In-Brain porn not being spent at grocery store), etc. Content couldn't be produced fast enough. Dudes no longer left basements, maxing out credit, arranging for intravenous feeding apparati (one recession-busting success story will be the huge feeding apparatus boom,) "soiled and stinking, but experiencing pleasure, pleased, retinal neurons fooling the lateral geniculate nucleus into experiencing complete stereoscopic perspective, full-on face-coding, legit world portrayal."

Kayla doesn't want to go. But the rent is due and life on the riotous streets isn't something she wants to experience firsthand. Against her better instincts and moral code Kayla goes with the man. As promised, he does nothing untoward after he's turned on the cameras and attached 32 electrodes to her. He lets her attach the more invasive electrodes herself.

Kayla mimes some motions. Sexual motions. Come-hithers. Ski-pole type wrist actions. Sultry reclines. Sucks a high-tech stick for eight minutes. Places a different high-tech stick inside her after disinfecting it herself. She hopes no one she knows experiences her VIB. There will be millions to choose from after all. She earns three months' rent in under an hour.

"Nice doing business with you. If you bring good-looking friends around I'll give you 10% of what I pay them," says Don Steel.

"Do you do mature?" Kayla asks, hoping to get work for her layabout mother, also an out-of-work actress, now that Kayla has mortgaged her moral code and all.

"Afraid not, demand is minimal, see. This guy does though," he says, and hands her the card of Todd Prolapse. "Does a wide-range of niche. Real wide. Wider than you might think. Might not be...well, I run a class operation here. I don't want to vouch for whatever might be going on at Todd Prolapse's at any given time. Certainly I have seen, ahem, equine things, things, scenes of an equine nature. I'm just saying, saying you ask me about mature, here's a guy I know does mature. Not vouching for Todd Prolapse outside of saying he does a lot of mature and he does a lot of stuff a little crazier than just mature if you know..."

Donny Steel then plugs her VIB program into the USB port at the back of his skull, places himself, penilely, in his totally optional but quite popular vagina-bag, closes his eyes, and enjoys a sex simulation with Kayla's recorded presence that's 99.3% similar to really doing it. Kayla checks her phone while this goes on.

"Not bad at all," says Don Steel to himself, smoking a cigarillo after. "A real tenderness, something elusive and good, if a little on the cellulitic side. Should be a hot seller."

Montage ahead a year and Kayla is shacked up with the millionaire Todd Prolapse. They're at the movies. At the concession stand he orders a $71 hot dog.

The initial retail instinct in the Verisimilitudinous In-Brain boom's wake was to lower prices on competing consumer goods like movies, hot dogs, umbrellas, etc. Problem was that consumers of crystal keel and adult VIBs weren't buying fries or umbrellas at any price, not even below cost to retailers. They just didn't care. They had what they wanted: A warm female to experience intimately; a jackbooted Nazi to kick their testicles; a football team to use the VIB user as celebratory receptacle.

So all companies except McDonalds and Wal-Mart will jack prices up to unreasonable levels so that the remaining sliver of puritanical non-VIB/keel addicts pay a premium for anything outside the basic staples of existence, which staples VIB-users still grudgingly purchase and fight through Soviet-style food-lines for at Wal-Mart and McDonalds.

Todd Prolapse never watches his own product, not even the Grand Canyon-y offerings he's CRTC-mandated to produce one of for every 15,000 pornographic VIBs he produces.

Walking toward their cinema, they bump into a familiar face.

"Goddamn if it isn't Don Steel," says Prolapse.

"Toilet Todd Prolapse," says Don Steel, Toilet Todd being Prolapse's nickname because of the unwholesome content he's unleashed on the lateral geniculate nuclei of the world. Prolapse being his legal surname, after he changed it from Swanberg.

"How's business?" asks Prolapse.

"Can't complain. You still doing Mega Tits Amputee? Had an inquiry the other day from a Mega Tits Amputee who stopped by the office, told her to look you up."

"Mega Tits Amp, Mature, Mummification, Muffled, Mirror, Milk, Mexican, Male-Dom, Mature in Gangbang, Megatits (general), Messy, Milk, Mask, and Malaysian my friend," says Todd

Prolapse, able to rhyme off so many M categories from memory because he's a crystal keel user, has only been using for five years, and it's still keeping him quite sharp.

Kayla notices that Todd repeats the *milk* category, but chooses to let it slide.

They arrange a meeting the next afternoon after Todd Prolapse 'steals some shots' at the Etobicoke Petting Zoo.

Later, Todd Prolapse puts on his Google Head and Googles the IVIBDB of Ron Steel, sees his grosses, his critical flops and successes. Prolapse then tries to mount Kayla for some IRL fornication, one of maybe only a few hundred couples in a developed nation still bothering with IRL stimulation.

"Take that thing off," Kayla says, "It creeps me out."

Before removing his Google Head, Todd Prolapse instructs it to play *Astral Weeks* by Van Morrison because that's their love-making record and something about its tones create the perfect rhythm for Prolapse to thrust to.

Kayla hates *Astral Weeks* and considers Prolapse's syncopated thrusts silly and insincere. She prefers to VIB it up with VIBs of various lifeguards who just go to town and don't thrust effeminately or with a wonky time signature.

They wake early in the morning to get to the petting zoo before children start arriving. Todd doesn't like to 'steal his shots' with children around, such is the ethical code Todd Prolapse lives by.

Todd wears a hoodie with the hood conspicuously up as he pays their $450 entrance fee. Todd doesn't realize this makes him resemble the Unabomber, whom the culture has by then largely forgotten, but still. Kayla, with no shot-stealing responsibilities, stands around looking bored.

When the farmer attends to his duties Todd gets out the high tech stick. He pets a lamb with the stick to acclimate lamb to stick, feeds the lamb feed from the dispenser. He applies an edible adhesive to the tip of his stick, attaches feed to stick's tip, gets the lamb to start licking the high-tech stick. He's approaching the sheep from a rearward angle when he freezes in his buggerous tracks.

"Standards and practices. Don't move."

These are the words Prolapse dreads. The reason he's at the petting zoo instead of his studio is that since the proliferation of sexualized quadrupeds, PETA had been all, "Hey, that sheep doesn't want your high-tech stick up his butt, please, Todd Prolapse." But market forces always speak louder than goopy activists, so the compromise is that only licensed owners could prostitute their pets and livestock. These licenses were meted out sparingly, allowing the owners of sexualized animals to charge outrageous prices, hence Prolapse's clandestine petting zoo efforts.

Prolapse puts his hands up, drops his high-tech stick, and prepares to face consequences. All to save a measly $10,000 and fatten his bestiality margins.

Kayla tries to walk away but is also apprehended. From the heights of Canadian sitcom success to this, she thinks.

In the squad car Special Agent Jergens heaps no shortage of scorn on Todd Prolapse.

"My father raised sheep," says Jergens, "Sheared the sheep. Sold the wool. That is the appropriate man/sheep relationship."

"Thanks for that," says Todd Prolapse.

"My own goddamn son is a VIB addict. Doesn't leave his room except during those five minute breaks."

For reasons not fully understood, one had to remove their VIB USB key every several hours or the brain would overheat and explode. This was learned the hard way by the pioneering engineers who first perfected the In-Brain experience and indulged in their primitive content to the point of head explosion. The experience was so pleasurable that even after the first couple engineers' heads exploded, subsequent engineers kept pushing the limits and having their own heads explode despite the dire example provided by predecessors.

Eventually the 11th engineer is like, "Okay, I'm going to limit myself to two hours and nothing more," and had it not been for his self-control VIBs may never have reached the market as all the engineers responsible for their design would have died of head explosions.

As the technology advanced, users could safely remain in their IB fantasy world for at least eight hours. Hardcore VIB addicts hate the five-minute cool down period. They become fidgety in the extreme. A shit-eating connoisseur might shit in the mouth of a family member or household pet, having slid that far down the rabbit hole of depravity. The rich often keep prostitutes from their favourite category on call to get through the five minutes. The real-world prostitutes are always a letdown though, because with VIBs you have it exactly as you want it.

Jergens continues, "I looked at my son's order history the other day. Hair-raising stuff Mr. Prolapse. I'll tell you, I sincerely wish I hadn't looked at that order history."

"Sounds like a real dirt bag."

"He was a fine young man until we let him get that USB slot. He tricked his mother by saying he wanted to climb Mt. Kilimanjaro, frolic through the Serengeti."

"Shouldn't have believed him."

"Hey, I watched porn on the Internet when I was a boy. We all did. I didn't know it had gotten so…"

"What were you into?"

"Todd, err, Mr. Prolapse, Mr. Prolapse in my day, a young man Googled something like 'naked lady,' no joke. First thing I Googled when my parents got the Internet in 97 was 'naked lady.' After that it was 'Jennifer Aniston Boobs.'"

"You never moved beyond that? Still relieving your personal tensions to fake images of Jennifer Aniston boobs?"

"Of course not. But animals? Prolapsed anuses. That is sick. You're poisoning young minds."

"Don't watch it myself. I consider myself the only pure and decent man in the industry," said Prolapse.

"Ha! Decent. This purveyor of sheep-fuck fantasies, decent."

Kayla laughs.

"Never use the stuff. Stick to my beautiful hard-bodied girlfriend," says Prolapse.

Kayla exhales audibly.

"You'll go down hard for this Prolapse," says Jergens.

"I can afford a good lawyer because your son buys my Ball Kicking VIBs."

"My son, I'll have you know, is into forced cuckolding. Doesn't even have a girlfriend, and he's into forced cuckolding. Explain that to me you fuckwhistle? Where does that instinct come from?"

"There's a major demographic overlap between cuckolding, forced and otherwise, with bi-sex cuckolding, interracial cuckolding, and you know where it all leads Jergens?"

"Shut your mouth!"

"Black Dick Worship."

The Black Dick Worship market is the only thing that keeps the NBA and NFL alive a few years into the VIB boom, and by 2019 it really has nothing to do with sport anymore, only the vague idea that a game was played sometime in the recent past by the black-cocked men lining up to feed the mouth of young Jergens or whoever else wanted to be gangbanged by an authentic pre-VIB athletic squad.

"My son does not worship black dicks."

"He will soon enough. Black dicks will be worshipped by him."

Jergens made some noises.

After being booked, Todd remembers his appointment with Don Steel and decides to kill two birds with one stone and use his one allotted Mind Skype to Mind Skype Don Steel.

Don Steel's pulse vibrates with the signifier of an incoming Mind Skype, so he puts on his AltaVista Head, AltaVista having made a minor comeback as an early producer of heads, apparently.

"Kayla and I are in a bit of a bind here. Minor scrape with the authorities. Technicality really. I have to ask you a favour."

"Jesus Todd, it wasn't underage was it?" asks Don.

The one niche that the culture remains diligent about prohibiting is ephebophiliac and pedophiliac porn. As if by funneling their energy into these standards they can overlook the goats and demons and swords in all the wrong places that proliferate daily. Every producer fears some girl with a fake ID, maybe an undercover S and P agent, maybe not, bringing down his whole setup and landing him in jail for a decade.

"You know I run a clean operation. Got caught sticking a sheep is all," says Jergens.

"Oh, well, believe me, no one knows better than me how these statists impede the progress of the honest businessman. I'll come bail you out."

Charles

What Charles liked to consider his first kiss came in 1996. His real first kiss was in 7th grade at a pop and chips party. But that tall, blond, sort of ugly girl had been depraved and damaged, even at twelve, and had stuck her tongue down his throat aggressively and then thrust his hand down her pants. Charles preferred not to count that time because that girl had been widely regarded as uncouth and perhaps even lousy or infested.

The time he did count took place at a wedding. Charles' father Charles Senior had quit drinking a few months previous, and these occasions were hard on him. Their family clung together like Arc-bound animals against the crashing waves of boozy high spirits all around them.

Charles was in the 8th grade, unathletic, but handsome in a thoughtful kind of way. He noticed the cut-out of a brown-skinned girl's face, his age, seated at the table behind them. Their eyes met. Charles got nervous and tore a wing off his broasted chicken. An inebriate slapped Charles Sr. on the back and asked where his drink was, not knowing Charles Sr. had become a teetotaler after a series of blackouts.

Charles made eye contact with the girl again, a solid .5 seconds this time. She smiled a perfect smile at him, revealing large, gleaming white centrals that for a split-second pressed into her bottom gum. The inadvertent sexuality of this made the girl's father uncomfortable enough to joke about all the smiling and eye contact and everyone at the girl's table laughed. Charles didn't look over for some time after that.

When the dancing started, without telling anyone what he planned to do, Charles got up and asked the girl to dance. Her face flushed with a sweetness Charles never can find with even the most laborious 'innocent teen webcam' searches, but will one day get some approximation of during the height of his VIB-addiction in the 'Young-looking but still totally legal' category.

They performed off-tempo fast-dance moves during the fast song, didn't talk much, and then both sat down.

Charles Sr. eyed a sweating Molson Canadian. Charles' mom Joanne also eyed the sweating Canadian and telepathically transmitted, "Don't do it," to Charles Sr. because no one needed to go through all that again, with the blackouts and falling down and setting a bad example for Charles and his sister, which sister would break down crying and ask "What's wrong with Dad?" because she was only seven and didn't grasp the sorrows of grain liquor and Molson Canadian.

When Seal's *Kiss from a Rose* played, Charles worked up the nerve to revisit the girl. The slow dance was nice because of the frottage going on with the girl's nascent breasts and Charles' own chest, his hands in the small of her back, her sugary scent in his olfactory receptors. As a result, he'd always set his VIB's scent settings as close to this smell as he could, but never could quite recreate it, even after buying all manner of esoteric and costly scent plug-ins and drivers.

"I'm Jessica," the girl said.

"Charles Didier."

"How do you know Sarah?"

"I don't really. My parents were friends with her mom."

"Stephen is my cousin," said Jessica.

Charles drank from a glass of Pepsi at an empty table and said, "Oh wow, I think that has alcohol in it."

Jessica drank some and said, "Just tastes like pop to me." Still, they drank the rest of it down and when they resumed dancing they were closer together.

"Want to go for a walk?" Charles asked, and then cringed inwardly, because the way he asked made it sound like he was getting ready for the big sex attack.

"I'll ask my mom."

After some minor familial discord she came back and said, "I have to be back in five minutes."

Outside, a petulant older girl said to them, "You two going to suck face?" Jessica was steamed and spent most of their walk saying things like, "The nerve of that girl," and, "I bet she's the real slut!"

They sat on the base of signage that identified Giovanni's Reception Hall. He took her hand. He leaned in and brushed his lips against her glossed ones. The very opposite of the downstairs face-sucking horror he'd endured the previous year. They kissed several more times. Soft, solitary kisses, no tongue considered or desired. She stopped abruptly when a car drove past, not wanting to be found out.

Dancing to the final songs, she wrote down the number of where she was staying. Charles left with his family, laid in the backseat of their Chevy Suburban, alive with something.

"Did you have a good time?" his mom asked.

"Oh ya. I really like that girl," he said, already envisioning his marriage to this Jessica.

"Is that your girlfriend?" his sister asked.

"Yes it is," Charles said.

"That's nice. You're a little young, but that's nice I suppose," said his mom.

He didn't sleep that night. The next day, because one of the songs they'd danced to had been *What a Wonderful World* by Louis Armstrong, he rented *12 Monkeys* on Laserdisc, because A) his parents had bought a laser disc player right during the dawn of DVDs and there was pressure to rent laser discs to justify the cost, so Charles was more likely to get a ride to the video store if he requested a laser disc instead of a video, and B) this was before Napster even and if you wanted to hear a song you either bought the CD or in this case rented a laser disc featuring it.

He called in the afternoon, but Jessica wasn't there. She was scheduled to leave the next day and return to her hometown ten hours away. Would this be the great romantic tragedy that rotted Charles and turned him into a Monster Porn-obsessed creep? It would not. As he watched a golden-era Simpsons' original broadcast, she called and asked to meet on the boardwalk. Charles ran outside where his dad was mowing a lawn that didn't need mowing.

"I need a ride to the boardwalk!" Charles shouted at the senior Charles over the mower's rumble.

"What the hell for?"

"To meet Jessica."

Charles Sr. understood a thing or two about wanting and needing, so without a lot of teasing or baloney he drove his son fifteen minutes to the boardwalk across from the Central Mall.

Hand-in-hand the pubescents walked. She told him what life was like in Woodstock, Ontario where she was from: the conservatism of the adults and how two pre-teens holding hands on a boardwalk would be a real no-no there. At one point Charles put his hand on her butt and she was fine with this. An old lady out for a stroll reprimanded them, but Charles just said sorry, and when they were past the old lady he put his hand right back.

In the Pavilion, which was like a low-end amphitheater across from the boardwalk, they kissed a little more passionately, and her hand at one point brushed his crotch. For years, when asked to list his sexual experiences, this putative 'handjob' led the pack, even if few peers believed of this beautiful girl from out of town, or if they did they insisted it was his cousin, and that he'd committed incest.

For a couple years the girl occupied a meaningful place in the pulsing adolescent heart of Charles, and was a subject of hope, and was a subject of reverie and late night fantasies of how they'd construct a life, and it being 1996 he wrote heartfelt letters and would receive her heartfelt responses a few weeks afterwards. As teenagers they started having other romantic opportunities, and given that they lived ten hours away, they forgot about each other.

Charles got the Internet in 1998. Like me, Special Agent Jergens, and everyone of that era, he Googled things like *Celebrity Skin*. While he did well enough romantically in high school, didn't lead the league or anything, but did better than most, he indulged at least a couple times a day. Nothing abnormal or excessive for a hormonal teenager. By college, well, it's the same old story. You start out a sweet kid brushing lips against glossy ones, you end up in a handicapped bathroom 4-5 times a day trying to keep your dopamine levels up. Further down the road you end up on the neuroreceptive end of the high-tech stick experience. Such is, was, and will be the sadness of the times.

Kayla St. Clair would go on to have twin daughters by Todd Prolapse, and the twin daughters or some early manifestation of them also appeared in our skywomb. Todd P. turned out to be not so bad of a father.

The skywomb travelled at least three kilometres east over Lake Ontario. As my personal consciousness began to unspool from the others', I became concerned the skywomb might break and we'd plummet into icy depths. But maybe that wouldn't be so bad. The pre-cognitive memories of everything that would happen in my life were not what I'd hoped for. One gross example was the amount of castration VIBs I would go on to consume.

It was our entire lives, but in the consensus reality recorded by watches and phones we were only enbubbled for eighteen minutes. When it was done Charles and I drove back past the native reservation, past the industrial redolence of the mill. Charles dropped me off and said, "Later man." I tried to message Amy on Facebook, but her profile picture was different now, and she was some kind of dentist, or dental technician, and not associated with Kayla St. Clair at all.

The next day we were back at the marketing firm, strange figures at the marketing firm now. Our third-eyes peeled back and open to the thoughts and auras of colleagues. We'd say inexplicable things that unnerved our colleagues, like "Here's to Don Steel" or "Long live Todd Prolapse" and then laugh with hysterical terror. People steered clear of our floor so long as we got our three-hundred words finished every day, which was fine by us. We never did write the e-book, and then Charles left the marketing firm because he felt proximity to me was making the whole third-eye phenomenon worse for him.

Attempts to contact Amy proved futile, probably owing more to our IRL past than any occult manifestation of her we might have experienced. The conclusion we reached before Charles left was that whatever version of her we encountered was on some different plane doing succubaen work of the most damaging magnitude, and not really Amy but just something hijacked from my subconscious, something probably only accessible to Charles because of his work with the energy.

Cloninger

Johnny Walton

He sat patiently in the sterile lobby. It was plain. It was blue
and white, with blue and white tile and blue and white chairs.
The art was old timey sailboats and beached dinghies, spaced
nicely between the blue porcelain planters housing fake Orchids. The anxiety in the air gave him the feel of a dentist's
office, but the Narraganset art and the other customers made it
feel like the waiting room of a high-end retirement community. He tried not to imagine the perverse septuagenarian orgies
that came to mind.

"Mr. Cloninger?" A plain woman with a stiff posture
checked his presence for what had to have been the twentieth
time. "I see you enjoying our Orchidaceae. Those are very special.
They're based loosely on O'Keeffe." Her small talk matched her
average tone, pace, and fashion sense.

"Yes, I can imagine that there is a noticeable difference between an O'Keeffe Orchid and a normal Orchid."

"Mr. Cloninger." Her flat-line voice said enough. But she
continued: "*You* are the sole reason you are here. Wait patiently
for a little longer, or wait impatiently for much longer."

He didn't have a comeback for her, so he proudly stared,
hoping she would look up from her paperwork.

She finally looked up only after he lost heart. She watched
him watching the Orchids do nothing. "Or did you have some-

where to be?" she asked. He found solace in that her comment took too long to seem witty.

His silence was all the answer she needed to go about her business, whatever that must have been.

He sat there quietly. Trying not to even think. He was more curious than anything, but the boredom was slowly killing even that sentiment. It felt like he had been there forever already.

"Excuse me, Mr. Cloninger?" It was a soft voice from another plain woman, dressed the exact same as the one before. "I'm Miss Quinn, I have a few questions for you."

"Yeah, shoot."

"Do you have all of your paperwork? The last six people were missing their 1365.3C forms. I don't know if someone is being clumsy on our side of the house or if I just got six bad apples in a row." She seemed genuinely concerned with this form.

He obliged and held out his manila folder. She read the name on the tab and bounced it off of a sheet of paper she had in her hand. She took the folder and thumbed through it for a moment. After moving a few pages around and reading the contents of the last one, she returned the folder, told him to stay put and walked behind the reception desk. A brief moment passed.

"Mr. Cloninger?" She called out from behind the desk, phone in hand.

"Yeah?"

"He's ready for you."

"Finally."

"There's no need for that, Mr. Cloninger. Come with me." She walked back out from behind the desk and into the sitting area.

"Come this way, please." She motioned and turned around a corner he hadn't noticed before.

He followed the plain woman down a hallway that seemed to go on forever. The blue and white wouldn't end. The halogen lights made the average art that much more bland.

"Alright, Mr. Cloninger, when you walk in, don't sit until you are invited to sit. And please don't get too emotional. I hate having to deal with that."

She stopped in front of a set of double doors. She gave him a once over, wiped some lint from his shirt and opened the door on the left.

He walked inside to find a simple office, modestly sized with a weathered IKEA desk. The man at the desk was on the phone, fidgeting with a pencil. He motioned towards the chair with an extended hand. Cloninger sat.

He tried to make himself comfortable, but the chair was too similar to those in the lobby and it was nearly impossible to get comfortable in a seated position. He looked around the small office at innocuous certificates, awards and a few pictures of what he presumed were family. The man across from him got off the phone with a quiet "I love you too." And put the pencil in a mug full of pencils that read "#1 DAD."

He smirked and said "I don't like pens. They are too permanent. Nothing is *that* permanent."

Cloninger was nonplussed.

#1 DAD was of an average build. His tie was about fifty years out of place and his sleeves were rolled about a third of the way up his arms. It appeared that he had pomade in his black hair and he smelled like cigarettes. He reminded Mr. Cloninger of his father.

"All right. Where to start? I take it you were treated well?"

"As well as can be expected, sir."

"Oh God! Let's drop that. It makes me sound so old."

"Your Honor, then?"

#1 DAD thought for a second. "It doesn't matter. Don't call me anything. This shouldn't take too long anyhow. Now, do you want to have a counselor present?"

"No, thank you."

"Good. You know, something we don't really tell people is that it doesn't help anyways. It just kind of... makes people feel better. And when it comes to that, I always say 'what the hell? Why not?' There is nothing I like more than to make people feel better."

"It would seem that way."

"So, do you understand where we are at, Mr. Cloninger?"

"Yeah. I went through the whole process. Mr. Cephas walked me through it, and went over everything. I have just been waiting on you for the bottom line." He sat quiet for a second, then added: "It wasn't really like I expected. I thought you would be more involved."

"Yeah, no shit huh? We really had to modernize around here. There just wasn't the infrastructure to keep up with the demand, so to speak. You want to know what made the biggest difference? The Rothschild Foundation. Honestly. Big help. But I *do* take this job seriously. I had to outsource a bulk of the menial stuff: you want to know how to say 'mountains of paperwork' in Hindi?" He laughed at his own joke. "It's funny, but most Indians don't do business with us, they use a totally different company. But seriously, I assure you, it is not much different than it used to be. We got Windows Vista a few years ago, and things are clicking along. Anything else?"

"No," Cloninger said. "It's all been said."

"And documented?"

"Yes, and documented."

"Good. I had a problem with that part in the recent past. People were not pulling their weight like they should have been. There's always someone trying to cut corners." He took a deep breath. "Okay then. There are like a million people waiting on me right now; last chance for any questions or comments."

"Is it like people say?"

He opened the folder back up and began to sign paperwork as he laughed a little. "Oh no. Not really. There's even a Republican Club. I swear you people make me laugh my ass off when I check in on you."

"Is there anything I could have done?"

"I mean, it's pretty cut-and-dry: shellfish, foreskins, and po-ly-blends." He looked intently at Cloninger for a few seconds. "The corridor you're looking for is out of my doors and on the left hand side."

"Ironic."

"Oh, yeah. That's a complete coincidence. Very few people pick up on that." He laughed a little. "It says as plain as daylight – 'HELL' – so just keep going straight until you hit the first set of double doors. Someone should be over there to help. I hope things work out for you. I really do wish sometimes that I had more con-trol over this part." He reached out a hand. Cloninger shook it.

"I always thought you would have more of a say in the outcome."

#1 DAD laughed again. "If I had a dime for every time someone told me that I wouldn't be in this little office all day, that's for Goddamn sure!"

About the Authors

Kevin Lee Peterson lives in Nashville, Tennessee, where he works in the wine industry. He is a graduate of Columbia University.

E. M. Stormo is a fiction editor by day, writer by night, and a teacher and promoter of musical literacy at all times. His recent work has appeared in The Conium Review, 404 Words, Pure Slush, and elsewhere.

A former economics professor, Steve Slavin earns a living writing math and economics books. His short story collection, *"To the city, with love,"* was recently published.

Tantra Bensko teaches fiction writing with UCLA Extension Writing Program. Her *Agents of the Nevermind* psychological suspense series explores social engineering through mind control, media theatrics, blackmail, bribery, false flags, hypnosis, secret societies, cults, and disinformation to convince the public of humanitarian motives for coups and proxy wars.
http://flameflower.wixsite.com/agentsofthenevermind

David Mathew is the author of twelve books, most recently *Ventriloquists, 0 My Days* and *Sick Dice* (all Montag) and two academic books entitled *Fragile Learning* and *The Care Factory*, which combine Higher Education and psychoanalysis. As a PhD holder, he works as an education developer for a UK university, his interests being psychoanalysis and issues of lifelong learning. As a writer of fiction, he favours dark and comic tales, and he is currently working on a commissioned novel entitled *Nostalgia's Boat* and an academic book entitled *Psychic River: Storms and Safe Ports in Lifelong Learning*.

Kenneth Levine's short stories have been published or accepted for publication in New Plains Review, Anak Sastra, Thuglit, Imaginaire, Skewed Lit, Jerry Jazz Musician, and an anthology entitled Twisted. He is the winner of a Jerry Jazz Musician short story contest and the featured writer in an Anak Sastra issue.

Connor de Bruler was born in Indianapolis, IN and grew up in lower Germany and upstate South Carolina. His first two novels (*Tree Black* and *The Mountain Devils*) were published by Montag Press. He has been published in several anthologies alongside authors like Joe R. Lansdale, Bentley Little, and Ethan Hawke. He lives in South Carolina.

Amanda Marbais' fiction has appeared in *Apalachee Review, Portland Review, The Doctor T.J. Eckleburg Review, Joyland, The Collagist, McSweeney's Internet Tendency* and many other journals. Her speculative fiction has appeared in *Lady Churchill's Rosebud Wristlet*, and her Noir fiction in *Thuglit*. She's the author of *A Taxonomy of Lies* (Bottlecap Press, 2016). She writes reviews for *Your Impossible Voice*. She lives in Chicago where she is the Managing Editor of *Requited Journal*. A special thanks to *Shirley Magazine* where *Fullness* first appeared.

Mike Sauve has written non-fiction for *The National Post, Variety, Exclaim! Magazine* and *HTML Giant*. His fiction has appeared in *McSweeney's* and elsewhere. His novels *The Wraith of Skrellman* and *The Apocalypse of Lloyd* are available from Montag Press.

Christopher Connor holds an MFA from Saint Mary's College of California. His story *The Last Best Place*, published in the Mid-American Review, was selected by Daniel Chacon as a 2014 AWP Intro Journals Project Winner.

This is Gray Oxford's writing debut at these rates. He was raised in North Carolina at any rate, and at considerable rates he now lives in the East Village. Gray dedicates this work to Cora who would cut off her sixth toe for love.

Marko Vignjević was born on the 9th of August, 1978. He lives and writes out of Belgrade, Serbia. His writing history includes The Premiere, Cycle No.1, a winner of the Zavetine Literary Award, and *Writings of a Wretch*, a vignette, published by Black Leaf in 2009.

Zachary Amendt was a 2015 Million Writers Award finalist for the title story in his debut collection, *Stay*. His stories have been featured in The Masters Review, Dzanc Books, Underground Voices, Phantom Drift and Saint Mary's Magazine. He is the author of *Liquidating Perry*, a recollection.

Johnny Walton lives in San Diego. He writes short fiction that has earned him such praise as "good job, son" and "maybe next time..." His last book, Moonlighter, made the Amazon top 100,000 for two weeks straight.

Connye Griffin is the author of nonfiction news articles, food and lifestyle blog posts, poetry, and now a tale imagining one dark branch of the human tree. She produces a food and lifestyle blog, OurEyesUponMissouri.com, which has been well-received and given birth to freelance, nonfiction opportunities in print and on-line publications. An original poem by Griffin has been featured in an anthology titled *Candles of Hope: A Collection of Cancer Poetry*, edited by Wendy Lawrence.

Trevor D. Richardson is the founder of The Subtopian, a regular writer and editor for the magazine, and the author of *American Bastards* from Subtopian Press. A west coast man by birth, Trevor was brought up in Texas and has since ventured back west and put down roots in Portland, Oregon. He has devoted his writing career to helping others find success by forming friendships and working relationships with other writers and artists. Trevor looks for ways to reach across media to other types of creative people to find that place where music, visual art, and literature intersect and is dedicated to creating a new market where new voices can thrive without sacrificing quality or principles. Trevor has written numerous short stories published in a variety of magazines including Word Riot, Underground Voices, and a science fiction anthology called *Doomology: The Dawning of Disasters*.

Made in the USA
Lexington, KY
14 March 2018